Sif and the Dwarfs' Treasures

ALSO BY
JOAN HOLUB & SUZANNE WILLIAMS

Don't miss the latest books in the
Goddess Girls series!
Medea the Enchantress
Eos the Lighthearted

Coming soon:
Clotho the Fate

Check out the most recent books in the
Heroes in Training series!
Dionysus and the Land of Beasts
Zeus and the Dreadful Dragon

Coming soon:
Hercules and the Nine-Headed Hydra

Read more books in the Thunder Girls series!
Freya and the Magic Jewel

Coming soon:
Idun and the Apples of Youth
Skade and the Enchanted Snow

Thunder Girls

BOOK 2

Sif and the Dwarfs' Treasures

**JOAN HOLUB &
SUZANNE WILLIAMS**

Aladdin

New York   London   Toronto   Sydney   New Delhi

ALADDIN

An imprint of Simon & Schuster Children's Publishing Division
1230 Avenue of the Americas, New York, New York 10020
First Aladdin paperback edition August 2019
Text copyright © 2018 by Joan Holub and Suzanne Williams
Cover illustration copyright © 2018 by Pernille Ørum
Interior illustration of tree copyright © 2019 by Elan Harris
Also available in an Aladdin hardcover edition.
All rights reserved, including the right of reproduction in whole or in part in any form.
ALADDIN and related logo are registered trademarks of Simon & Schuster, Inc.
For information about special discounts for bulk purchases, please contact
Simon & Schuster Special Sales at 1-866-506-1949 or business@simonandschuster.com.
The Simon & Schuster Speakers Bureau can bring authors to your live event. For more
information or to book an event contact the Simon & Schuster Speakers Bureau
at 1-866-248-3049 or visit our website at www.simonspeakers.com.
Designed by Laura Lyn DiSiena
The text of this book was set in Baskerville.
Manufactured in the United States of America 0719 OFF
2 4 6 8 10 9 7 5 3 1
The Library of Congress has cataloged the hardcover edition as follows:
Names: Holub, Joan, author. | Williams, Suzanne, 1953- author.
Title: Sif and the dwarfs' treasures / by Joan Holub and Suzanne Williams.
Description: First Aladdin hardcover edition. | New York : Aladdin, 2018. |
Series: Thunder Girls ; 2 | Summary: Twelve-year-old Sif, goddess of the harvest and a
reluctant seer whose abilities are woven into her hair, goes on a quest with Freya and Loki
after Loki cuts her hair in a prank gone wrong, causing the crops of Midgard to fail.
Identifiers: LCCN 2018008180 | ISBN 9781481496438 (hardcover) |
ISBN 9781481496445 (eBook)
Subjects: | CYAC: Mythology, Norse—Fiction. | Friendship—Fiction. | Hair—Fiction. |
Dwarfs (Persons)—Fiction. | Oracles—Fiction. | Goddesses, Norse—Fiction. |
Loki (Norse deity)—Fiction. | Freya (Norse deity)—Fiction. | BISAC: JUVENILE
FICTION / Legends, Myths, Fables / Norse. | JUVENILE FICTION / Girls & Women. |
JUVENILE FICTION / Social Issues / Friendship.
Classification: LCC PZ7.H7427 Sc 2018 | DDC [Fic]—dc23
LC record available at https://lccn.loc.gov/2018008180
ISBN 9781481496421 (pbk)

For our fantastic readers.
Knowledge is power!

Amelia G., Andrade Family, Kira L., Ellis T.,
Jenny C., Lorelai M., McKenna W., Evilynn R., Haidi S.,
Piper R., Daniele R., Lily-Ann (Red) S., Latoya S.,
Reese O., Serenity J., Madison M. and MacKenzie M.,
Christine D-H., Olive Jean D., Iris L.,
Brittany P., Sienna W., Caitlin R., Hannah R., Sarah M.,
and you.

—J. H. and S. W.

Contents

1	RUNES CLASS	1
2	PODMATES	19
3	BOYGODS	40
4	THOR	56
5	THE HEARTWOOD LIBRARY	80
6	THE DREAM	99
7	CAUGHT!	112
8	LAND OF THE DWARFS	133
9	THE BET	151
10	JUDGMENT	176
11	LOFN	208
12	ONE LAST GIFT	222
	AUTHORS' NOTE	235
	ACKNOWLEDGMENTS	239
	GLOSSARY	241

Sif and the Dwarfs' Treasures

1
Runes Class

TWELVE-YEAR-OLD SIF PULLED A HANDFUL of thumb-size stone tiles from a small cloth bag and placed them on the floor in front of her. The girl-goddess frowned at the angular symbols carved into their surfaces. Other students in her fourth-period Runes class were also studying tiles they'd taken from the cloth bag when it had been passed around the room. Sif's eyes darted left and then right. She couldn't help noticing that kids nearby seemed to be having an easy time with today's assignment. Well, she wasn't!

If she had a choice, she wouldn't even be taking this class. However, everyone's classes had been assigned two weeks ago, when they'd all first arrived at Asgard Academy. She worried that requesting a change might cause the formidable Odin, coprincipal of AA with his wife, Ms. Frigg, to question her abilities. To wonder if they'd made a mistake in inviting her here. Plus, Ms. Frigg was actually *teaching* the class!

Odin had created this special school right after the famous war between the worlds of Asgard and Vanaheim had ended. The academy had been established to try to "promote better relationships and mutual understanding among all nine of the Norse worlds." These worlds were located on three enormous, ring-shaped levels stacked one above the other, with three worlds to each ring.

Some students from each of the nine worlds had

been invited (well, ordered, really) to attend the new academy. Odin had summoned girlgoddesses and boygods from Asgard and Vanaheim, plus dwarfs, lightelves, frost giants, humans, and other beings. Pretty much everyone who'd been invited had come, except the dreaded fire giants, that is!

A sudden brisk breeze blew in through the open windows of the classroom, which was named Fensalir Hall. *Brr!* Built of logs and topped by a steep, slanted roof of overlapping triangular wooden shakes, the hall was one of many within the academy. Shifting to sit cross-legged in her place among the circle of students seated on the classroom's wood floor, Sif caught a glimpse of huge leaves outside the window. These grew from the ginormous World Tree, named Yggdrasil, which protected the nine worlds. Like all the classrooms at AA, Fensalir Hall magically hovered high within that ash tree's branches.

Sif tucked the hem of the linen shift she wore beneath her navy-blue *hangerock* (an apronlike wool overdress) under her knees for warmth. Then she stared at her eight tiles again and tried to make sense of them. Their symbols shifted around crazily as she studied them, sometimes appearing upside down and other times facing the wrong direction. They weren't really moving. It was her *mind* that was mixing things up, as usual. No one else at the school had this same problem with rune-letters, as far as she knew. And she wasn't about to reveal her difficulty to anyone!

Ms. Frigg looked up from her chair at the center of the circle, where she sat knitting an orange-and-white ruffled sock. Or maybe it was a hat? Hard to tell. Anytime she had a few minutes, she was always knitting. Mostly gifts for other people, like for instance, the ear warmers she'd made for some dwarfs that the girlgoddess Freya had encountered recently. The teacher spun the most beautiful, strong yarn in all the worlds and gave her creations away generously. Everyone cherished her kind gifts, even if they did turn out a little, um, quirky.

Ms. Frigg flipped back the single long blond braid that hung forward over one of her shoulders. "I'll give you all a few more minutes," she told the class. As coprincipal of the academy, she kept pretty busy with day-to-day school stuff, while Odin oversaw the well-being of all nine worlds from a perch at the top of Yggdrasil. Fourth-period Runes was the only class Ms. Frigg taught.

"Don't forget," she went on. "While I expect you always to do your best thinking, prophecy is more of an . . ." She paused, waiting for the class to finish her sentence.

"More of an art than a science," Sif and the other students dutifully replied. It was something their teacher reminded them of almost every class. It meant that prophecy, unlike science, was often based on sketchy information. So you had to use guesswork, guided by gut feelings, to make prophetic connections with the runes—as in, use them to see into the future.

However, before doing any of that, Sif would need to actually *read* the runes carved on her dumb tiles. And that was a struggle for her.

She twisted a strand of her waist-long golden hair around one finger and fought down panicky feelings as she tried to make sense of the symbols before time was up. Her hair was her pride and joy, the source of her goddess powers, and also her best feature. Some compared its color to that of ripe wheat. Fitting, since she was the girlgoddess of bountiful harvests. Right now, though, she kind of wished she were the girlgoddess of expert rune reading!

The symbols on her tiles surprised her by abruptly settling down and righting themselves. As sometimes happened for no reason at all, her mind had stopped scrambling them. She read the symbols quickly, just in case they started wiggling again. *Hmm.* They spelled the runeword *mjollnir.*

What a relief to have solved *that* mystery! But she

now faced a new challenge. A word definition. Because *mjollnir* could mean several things. Most often, it was associated with the verbs "grind" and "crush."

When Sif checked the circle of students to see how others were doing, her eyes landed on Thor, who sat directly across from her. The red-haired boygod was the biggest and strongest kid in the whole school. And his already incredible strength was *doubled* by the magic belt he wore, which everyone called his Belt-o'-Power. The large, oval gold buckle at the heavy belt's middle was engraved with the rune for *T*, which stood for "Thor," of course.

Just then he looked up and met her gaze. She quickly looked away.

This wasn't the first time their eyes had met. Not that she looked at him often! She looked at *lots* of people. It was only that Thor always seemed to be looking at her at the exact same moment her eyes (accidentally) settled on him.

Suddenly a boygod sitting right beside her recrossed his legs, kicking her tiles and sending them skidding halfway across the floor under the teacher's chair. "Oops, sorry," he said with an impish grin. "My bad."

Sif glared at the black-haired, blue-eyed boy. She was pretty sure his scattering of her tiles hadn't been an accident. He sometimes did stuff like this to her and other students for no other reason than to stir things up. If only Ms. Frigg had noticed this time! However, the teacher's chair was angled slightly away from the two of them.

"You did that on purpose, Loki!" Sif accused softly. The boygod of fire, who was a shape-shifter, too, was as spontaneous and unpredictable as . . . well . . . *fire*. He wasn't one of the fire giants, though, thankfully. No one she knew had ever actually seen one of those.

Loki's grin widened. "Sorry," he said, not looking sorry at all. "I'm done with my runes and bored. Hey, watch this." He glanced over at Ms. Frigg, who now appeared to be counting the stitches along one knitting needle. While she was distracted, he leaped up.

In a flash he darted behind the teacher, scooped up all eight of Sif's scattered tiles, then was back in mere seconds. "Here you go," he said with a charming, mischievous smile. He dropped the tiles into the palm of her hand.

Many girls found Loki cute, and Sif supposed he was, with his dark-blue eyes and the way his longish black hair curled up a bit at the back of his neck. But she believed that a person's behavior, not his appearance, was what made him attractive. Like in the saying "Handsome is as handsome does."

"How'd you do that?" she asked, nodding toward the path he'd just run.

"Magic shoes!" he replied. Sticking his legs straight out in front of him, he gestured to his feet. It was only then that Sif noticed the bright-yellow shoes he was wearing today. "With these babies, I can race like the wind over land and water. And I can also escape a teacher's notice when I want to." He grinned. "I named them Yellow Fellows."

Sif tried not to laugh at the silly name, but she couldn't help giggling a little. Despite his troublemaking ways, there was no denying that Loki could be entertaining!

Still, he was causing her to waste precious time. "Back to work," she muttered. She quickly arranged her tiles in order again. She'd spent so much time deciphering her rune-letters that she had little left for pondering what event her runeword might foretell.

Ironically, despite her reading difficulties, she actually had some talent with prophetic predictions. She mostly kept that information to herself, though. Because in the past her talent at divining the future had caused her nothing but trouble!

"Trouble?" asked a girl named Angerboda, nosily leaning over to study Sif's runes. The girl was a frost giant and so could make herself grow five times normal-girl size if she wanted to. Which was often the case whenever she got mad! Like Loki, who was half-giant himself, she was a troublemaker.

"Huh?" Sif replied, thinking Angerboda had read her mind or something. But then she realized that the girlgiant had only been asking if Sif was having trouble reading her tiles.

"No," Sif said, cupping her tiles closer with her hands.

Her talent at prophecy had been revealed long ago by a wandering fortune-teller named Völva, who'd visited Sif's home village at the outskirts of Asgard. Though Sif had been barely three years old at the time, Völva had recognized her potential and told her parents of it. They had encouraged Sif's ability. So, proudly, Sif had begun blurting out every single prophecy that came into her mind.

And some of them had embarrassed or hurt others. Like the time she told a beautiful lady, "You will get a wart on your nose." Or the time she told a much older girl at school, "Your BFF will start crushing on your boyfriend." Before long she'd gotten the kenning

11

(a hyphenated nickname) of fortune-*tattler* instead of fortune-*teller*. The final straw had involved a fortune-tattling, er, fortune-*telling* rune experiment gone dreadfully wrong. This had happened in second grade, and she'd wound up hurting, and ultimately losing, a very good friend.

Not wanting to think about that, Sif pushed it out of her mind. Still unable to figure out the meaning of her own runes, she glanced over at Loki's six carefully lined-up tiles. For whatever reason, it took only a few moments this time for the rune-letters on them to stop swimming and hold steady for her. Sometimes it happened that way—if she was lucky.

"*Klippa,*" she read aloud. The word meant "to clip or cut." "You can clip or cut a lot of things," she mused. "What do you think it means?"

Loki gave a little start, as if she'd caught him by surprise. Then his eyes took on a hooded look. "Who knows?" he said evasively.

Why was he acting so secretive? Sif wondered.

"Time is up." Ms. Frigg put down her knitting and stood from her chair. "Who would like to share their work?"

One by one, students began sharing aloud their rune-words' meanings and suggesting prophecies that might be connected to them. "Mine's *atlaga*," announced a boy-dwarf named Alviss. "Means 'attack.' Pretty sure it's a foretelling of coming trouble from enemies of Asgard."

Since grown-up frost giants were constantly trying to breach the newly repaired wall that surrounded Asgard (a wall that had nearly been destroyed during the Asgard-Vanaheim war), this prophecy was likely accurate. Several students shot uneasy glances at Angerboda. Like them, Sif sometimes suspected that the frost giant students at AA might be plotting trouble just like their grown-up relatives.

As others spoke up about their runes, Sif kept her hand down. If Ms. Frigg eventually called on her anyway, she planned to say as little as possible. Since Loki loved to be the center of attention, she was surprised that he kept quiet too. He'd even jumbled up his tiles already.

"My runeword is *uggligr*," Thor told everyone when Ms. Frigg called on him. "Since it means 'dreadful,' I think it's a warning that we can expect the fire giants or the frost giants to do *dreadful* things in the future."

"Yeah, like *attack* us!" Alviss blurted out.

"You never know," Angerboda said, smiling smugly.

Alviss and Thor exchanged a grim glance as a murmur of concern swept the classroom. Looking to settle old scores, giants and trolls—not all, but some—were a constant threat.

"Attacks are always possible, but no one should be worried. Our security is top-notch, including our new wall," Ms. Frigg assured the class.

As she bent to help another student with his rune-letters, Loki began drumming his fingers against the

14

floor. Was he feeling anxious about the idea of invading giants? Sif wondered.

She soon discovered the answer was no. Instead, as usual, his mind was fixated on making mischief. Now that the teacher's attention was focused elsewhere, he took the opportunity to say, "You know, another meaning of the runeword *uggligr* is 'ugly.'" He looked around the room and grinned, adding, "Like Thor's face." Then he cracked up laughing.

What?! Thor might not be as handsome as some boys, but he was *not* ugly! Sif sat up straighter, annoyed by Loki's mean joke. Loki had spoken plenty loud enough for Thor to hear, though not loud enough for his words to reach the teacher. Why, oh, why did he like to push Thor's buttons like this? Everyone knew Thor was hot tempered when provoked. (Such stormy behavior was actually kind of fitting, since he was the boygod of storms.) This time Loki had gone too far.

In an instant Thor was across the room, his fists balled

to punch Loki out. Before he could follow through, however, Loki shape-shifted into fire.

"Yow!" Thor leaped back, blowing on his singed fingers to cool them. As Loki shifted back to his boygod form, Thor glowered at him. "I'll get you for that!"

Loki just laughed. "You and what army, Mr. Stormy-Pants?" he taunted as Ms. Frigg sternly separated the two boys.

Thor didn't *need* an army, Sif figured. With his strength and his Belt-o'-Power, he was practically an army of one. She watched him as, red-faced, he struggled to rein in his anger at Loki's insults. She wished Loki could manage the self-control not to tease others. And that Thor could find the self-control to direct his superstrength without anger!

And that's when a hazy prophecy regarding her runeword, *mjollnir*, began to form in her head. She sensed that *someone* among the students—maybe Loki or Thor, or maybe her or someone else—would soon acquire a new means to fight off any troublemaking giants. A means that would keep Asgard even safer. And that would be a very good thing!

Still, she didn't raise her hand to share this prophecy. Why not? Well, after the Horrible Thing that had happened in second grade, she didn't quite trust herself. What if she accidentally said (or did!) something that wound up hurting someone else . . . again? No, it was safer to let events play out without her interference. Even if she was pretty sure her prophecy was on the right track.

Suddenly a long, loud blast rang out. *Tooot!* It was the horn signaling the end of the period. At last! Just one more class and she'd be done for the day. Then, since today was Friday, the weekend could officially begin.

"Everyone may go except for Thor and Loki," Ms. Frigg announced.

Uh-oh, thought Sif as she rose to her feet. Those two were sure to get a lecture about their behavior. She didn't feel a bit sorry for Loki, only for Thor. Because in her humble opinion, Loki was the guilty party. Thor was merely his victim! Before leaving Fensalir Hall with the rest of the students, she sent the red-haired boygod a sympathetic glance. Thor caught her look and smiled back.

2
Podmates

AT THE END OF HER FIFTH-PERIOD TREE
Lore class, Sif shivered in the cold air as she stepped
outside the classroom. The school week was over, and
she didn't have any homework. Hooray! A light snow
was falling, so she flipped up the hood of her gray cloak
before scurrying across a woven fernway and darting
through a branch tunnel. Ten minutes later she reached
Vingolf Hall, the girls' dorm.

Once through the hall's outer door, she pulled off

her damp boots and placed them on a rack in the mudroom. Then she pushed through the inner door and into Vingolf. She nodded hi to some girls who were gathered at small tables scattered around the enormous, round communal room to talk, do homework, or play games. At the very center of this main part of the dorm was a fire pit, which vented through a hole in the ceiling.

Sif warmed her hands near the fire for a couple of minutes before padding in her thick wool socks to the sleeping pod she shared with three other girlgoddesses. There were eighteen such pods spaced all around the edge of the circular dorm, each one poking outward from the main communal space like the petals on a humongous flower. Some pods slept as many as eight, while others slept fewer.

Each group of podmates had named themselves at the beginning of school, things like the Shooting Stars, the Northern Lights, and the Polar Bears. The cute sign on the door of Sif's pod read: THUNDER GIRLS. That was the name she and her three podmates had chosen. It was a nickname that Heimdall, the Asgard Academy security guard, had given them. He had keen hearing, and one day, annoyed at the noise they'd been making while thundering around in their snow boots, he'd called them that name. Instead of taking offense, the girls had decided they liked—no, *loved* it. Thunder was powerful, after all, and to them the nickname signified girl power—which they definitely had!

Although most Vingolf pods contained girls from the same world, the four Thunder Girls were different. Freya was from Vanaheim. Sif and Idun were from Asgard. And Skade was a half-giant who'd grown up spending time in both Asgard and Jotunheim. She could enlarge to only half the height of regular giants such as Angerboda.

"Ow!" As Sif entered her pod, she tripped over one of Skade's boots, stubbing her toe. That girl had a dozen pairs of boots at least! Sif and their other podmates,

Freya and Idun, were constantly tripping over them, because Skade often forgot to leave her boots on the racks by the outer doors. Instead she'd shuck them off inside the pod and leave them lying wherever they fell.

Freya sat up in her podbed, a six-foot-long hammock made from one of Yggdrasil's seedpods. She watched Sif hop around on one foot holding her hurt foot in both hands. Wearing only her linen underdress, the girlgoddess had been lying on her back, reading a runebook. The illustration on its cover showed a wooden woman with flowing hair—a ship's carved figurehead. From the cover, Sif guessed that the book was for Norse History class.

"You okay?" Freya asked. The light coming in through the room's only window made the natural silver glitter in her pale-blond hair shimmer. All the Vanir (which was what the goddesses and gods of Vanaheim were called) had flecks of silver in their hair that glittered when caught by light, like dozens of tiny winking stars!

"Yeah, fine." Sif leaned one hand on the wall for balance. Rubbing her foot, she called out sweetly, "Hey, kitties."

In response, Freya's two gray tabby cats raised their heads to look over at Sif, before snuggling more tightly together at the end of Freya's podbed and purring more loudly. Though they were currently the size of regular cats, they were magical and could enlarge to pull Freya's flying cart. And whenever necessary, Freya could shrink them and the cart down to a cat's-eye marble, which she kept in a small leather pouch, one of several pouches that dangled from the many necklaces she always wore. Mostly, the tabby cats spent lots of time hanging out in Vingolf Hall, though, like now.

"No parties tonight? Where is everyone?" Sif asked, noticing that their other two podmates weren't around. She hung her gray wool cloak on the reindeer antler coatrack nailed to the back of their pod door. She was kind of surprised that Freya wasn't out in the hall's

23

common area, since she liked hanging out and making friends more than just about anything. And that girl could turn practically any activity into a party. Homework party. Snack party. Jewelry-making party (her favorite kind, since she loved jewelry). Which was pretty great, since these parties helped all four Thunder Girls befriend other students.

And that was exactly what Principal Odin wanted, of course. For students from each of the worlds to mingle and make friends. He wished them to understand and appreciate everyone's differences, in hopes that their example would lead the way in promoting harmony between all nine worlds. So far, except for Freya's parties, everyone in the dorms had pretty much stuck to their own groups, though. Hopefully this would change in time.

Freya set her book aside and swung her feet over the edge of her podbed, looking pleased to have company. "Not sure where Idun is, but Skade left to go shopping at Midgard Mall." She grinned, her pale-blue eyes spar-kling. "Get this—for new boots."

"Noooo!" Sif made a face of pretend horror. "As if we need more of those trip-hazards of hers around here!"

Freya giggled as Sif nudged the offending boot that had tripped her up earlier against the pod wall, where it would be more out of the way. "In fact," Sif went on, "maybe you should hold a boot-trading party so Skade could get rid of some of the ones she already has."

"Yeah, but you know she'd just trade for different boots," said Freya, making them both laugh.

Sif's hair had gotten a bit tangled during the day, so she fished a small mirror from the pocket of her *hangerock*, grabbed her comb, and started running it through her hair. In the mirror's reflection she saw Freya watching her. "Hey! I have an even better idea than a boot-trading party," Freya announced suddenly. "Let's have a hairstyling party! For you!"

"Huh? Oh, I'm not sure," Sif began, tucking her mirror away.

Quickly Freya reached for the book she'd been reading. Still on her podbed, she paged through it and then showed Sif a picture of a beautifully carved mermaid figurehead. The mermaid's hair was a mass of thin braids that looped every which way. "This style would look fabulous on you. And even if you decide you don't like it, you can always comb it back out."

Still, Sif hesitated. Her golden hair was her pride and joy. And she'd always worn it long and straight, or else in a simple ponytail, often adorned with ribbons, barrettes, headbands, clips, or decorative combs.

"C'mon. It'll be fun. Promise!" Freya urged.

"Well . . . okay," Sif said at last, allowing herself to be convinced. She hadn't known Freya all that long, so she didn't want to turn down her friendly offer. Doing fun stuff together with her podmates (and hopefully other girls too) would help them become better buds.

And that was exactly what Odin wanted for them all.

"Yes!" Freya exclaimed, excitedly pumping one fist. "Be right back!" She jumped down from her hammock-like podbed, causing it to sway. Startled, her cats leaped out of it. They hit the floor, then padded around a moment before jumping back into the bed. They found a warm spot, then curled up to nap again.

Meanwhile, Freya ran out into the dorm's common area and returned with a stool, which she now set in the center of their podroom. "Sit!" she commanded Sif playfully, pointing at the stool. Smiling nervously, Sif sat.

Freya fetched a large silver-backed hand mirror from the small closet beside her podbed and handed it to Sif. "Here. So you can watch your amazingly stupendous transformation." She traded the mirror for the comb Sif was holding. The latter was made of reindeer antler, just like their pod's coatrack. The comb's carefully sawed-out teeth had been fastened with small bronze nails to a backbone etched with a delicate pattern of thin, dark cross-hatching.

Sif watched in the mirror as the comb touched her shining golden hair. Gleefully, Freya separated various strands and began to weave them into many small braids. She asked lots of questions as she wove Sif's hair, and Sif had a feeling this was to try to make her less nervous about all this hair stuff. It worked, too. The minutes flew by as the two girls giggled and chatted merrily about classes and teachers.

Soon she found herself telling Freya about *mjollnir*, the runeword she'd created in Ms. Frigg's class. "It's related to the verbs 'grind' and 'crush.' What do you think it could mean prophecy-wise?" Sif asked.

Freya shrugged. "Hard to say. What do *you* think?"

Abandoning her usual caution, Sif said, "I was thinking it might foretell the future discovery of some new way of *crushing* enemy giants. Probably in a fighting situation. And that it might be related to *someone*—

it could be anyone, really, like possibly Thor or—"

"Wow! Interesting!" interrupted Freya, pausing in the midst of her braiding.

Uh-oh, thought Sif. She hadn't meant to tell anyone her guesses about the meaning of *mjollnir.* It was just that Freya was so easy to talk to, and the girl had a true gift for seeing the future, so her ideas on the runeword could prove helpful.

In the mirror she could see Freya eyeing her curiously now. It made her squirm around on the stool a little. She hoped Freya hadn't somehow guessed that Sif was a seer too. Though it was hard and not much fun keeping that ability a secret all the time, it seemed for the best. She didn't want to harm anyone with her so-called talent ever again!

Finally Freya spoke. "Prophecies can be tricky," she said, beginning to braid again. "I mean, you could be right." The mirror reflected her gentle smile. "Or it's possible your interpretation could be wishful thinking."

29

Huh? Freya's seeming doubt of Sif's seeing abilities stung a little. But then, Sif had been careful not to let anyone at AA know she *had* prophesying abilities, so why *wouldn't* Freya doubt her?

Besides, it wasn't like her seeings were always correct. There had been the Horrible Thing involving her best friend, for example. She'd also seen other things that hadn't come to pass—at least not in the *exact* way she'd expected. Like Ms. Frigg was fond of reminding everyone in Runes class, prophecy was an art, not a science.

"We'd all like Asgard to be safer from giants," Freya went on in a kind voice. In the mirror, Sif watched her begin to loop and pin the braids she'd woven into a dramatic style that approximated the figurehead mermaid's hairdo.

"True," murmured Sif. She really *was* concerned for Asgard's safety. But was Freya hinting that she had simply made up a prophecy she *hoped* would come true? No way!

"You are going to love this new hairtsyle," Freya enthused.

Sif turned the mirror from side to side to see better what was happening. But instead of sharing Freya's enthusiasm, she only grew alarmed at the sight of her hair. To her, the jumble of braids on her head just looked *wrong*. Cute for someone else. Way too fussy for her.

"Also, I find it *verrry* interesting that you think your prophecy might involve Thor," Freya went on as she unlooped some of the braids and then relooped them even more wildly.

"So?" said Sif. In the mirror she saw that a twinkle had come into Freya's pale-blue eyes.

"So I've seen you two looking at each other."

"Nuh-uh. When?" Sif said, feeling her cheeks grow warm.

"Lots of times. On the way to class. Eating in the V," Freya replied, referring to the Valhallateria, AA's dining hall.

Freya stepped from behind Sif and wagged a playful finger at her face. "I think maybe you're *crushing* on each other. As in *mjollnir*?"

"What? No!" Sif exclaimed, her cheeks growing warmer still. Freya had purposely emphasized the word "crushing" because she thought Sif's runeword might mean the liking kind of 'crush'! But that interpretation couldn't be right! "Thor and I have never even *talked* to each other!" Sif protested.

"Crushes often start with just looking," Freya said with a knowing grin.

Sif frowned. "No way are Thor and I crushing on each other. That isn't what my runeword means," she insisted. "Maybe you've just got love on the brain, since you're the girlgoddess of love and beauty."

"Maybe. Maybe not." Freya laughed good-humoredly, and Sif watched her brush her fingers over her favorite necklace. Made from hammered gold in a fancy design, it was decorated with winking rubies and diamonds. At the necklace's center dangled a large, teardrop-shaped jewel named Brising. Freya used this magical jewel to do her own future-tellings, which were usually correct. It was valuable and had been stolen twice recently, once by some dwarfs and another time by Loki. Which probably explained why Freya touched it now and then—to make sure it was still there.

Desperate to change the crushing subject, and having been thinking about Freya's necklace, Sif blurted, "I never told you before, but I *knew* Loki would steal Brising."

When Freya's grin vanished immediately, Sif wished she could take back her words. But it was too late. Looking both angry and hurt, Freya stood over her with her hands on her hips. "You mean he *told* you he planned to steal it? And you didn't tell *me*?"

"No!" Sif hastened to say. She leaped from her stool to stand facing Freya. "I . . . um . . . saw him steal it in a dream," she explained, shifting from foot to foot. Well, now she'd done it. The cat (and not one of the ones on Freya's podbed) was out of the bag.

Freya's eyes widened. "Like a *prophetic* dream? Are you saying you're a seer?"

"No! Um, maybe. Well, sort of, I guess," Sif admitted. She laid the hand mirror on top of the stool and began to pace back and forth. She could feel the new braids moving on her head. They felt weird, like ropes. So not her! "Only, I'm usually terrible at it," she went on. "I can't always tell the difference between a normal dream and a prophetic one, for one thing. That's why I didn't tell you about that dream. It could've been wrong and caused trouble."

She'd been pretty sure at the time that the dream about Freya's necklace was a prophetic one, though—because it had been so vivid. Her most vivid dreams almost always came true! The real reason she'd said nothing was because of her vow to keep her talent a secret after that disaster with her second-grade best friend.

Freya let out a huff. "You still should have told me."

Sif nodded. "I'm really sorry. At least you did get Brising back."

"Yeah," said Freya, starting to calm down. Suddenly she gasped, staring in the direction of their door.

Idun had arrived. She was all sweaty, her long brown hair was a wild mess, and the hem of her linen underdress was caked with dirt. "What happened to you?" the two girls asked at the same time.

"It was awful!" Idun said breathlessly as Sif snatched the hand mirror from the stool so the distressed girl could sit. "I'd just finished picking a boxful of apples for the Valhallateria. And I was on my way to drop them off at the V kitchen when, you'll never guess—an eagle zoomed down and swiped one of them!"

Idun, the girlgoddess of youth, was responsible for picking the deliciously sweet golden apples that kept all the goddesses and gods healthy and youthful. Her special apples grew year-round, even in winter snow, in one particular grove in Asgard. Though students often ate them whole, the V kitchen staff also made the apples into applesauce, apple juice, and baked goods such as apple cake and apple turnovers.

"So naturally, I ran after the eagle," Idun went on. "But then I tripped over a rock and fell into a big mud puddle, spilling my whole basket."

"Oh, poor you," Freya said sympathetically.

Idun nodded and shifted her weight on the stool. "Then while I was gathering up the spilled apples, the eagle landed on a tree branch above me." She hesitated before adding, "I swear it grinned at me the whole time it was eating that stolen apple. Like it was laughing at me and daring me to do anything about it. I wasn't about to get near that sharp beak, though!"

Freya and Sif exchanged looks. "Loki!" they said at the same time.

"In disguise," added Sif. Loki was a shape-shifter, after all. And stealing one of Idun's precious apples was the kind of annoying thing he would do, even though he could eat them anytime he wanted in the Valhallateria.

Idun drew in a sharp breath, guessing their meaning. "That eagle?"

Freya nodded. "It would be just like him to do it. He always does whatever he wants. And he never worries about anyone else's feelings."

"Exactly! Today he messed up my tiles in Runes class," said Sif. "And he teased Thor."

Sif looked up to see Freya staring at her with that knowing look again. Because she'd mentioned Thor? Talk about a one-track mind!

But it had been super mean of Loki to pick on shy, sweet Idun. She was kind to everyone and never said a bad word about him or anyone else. She was the last person anyone should want to hurt. The more Sif thought about it, the madder she got.

Abruptly changing the subject, Idun said to Sif politely, "I like your hair."

"Thanks," said Sif. She had a feeling that Idun didn't

think it suited her at all and was only being her usual nice self.

Then, without warning, Idun's face crumpled. She reached down, pulling up the hem of her underdress to reveal a scrape that was still bleeding a little. "I skinned my knee when I fell."

"Ooh! That looks like it hurts," sympathized Sif.

"C'mon. I'll help you wash and bandage it," Freya said quickly. Nodding, Idun headed for the washroom across the hall. Freya started to follow, then paused in the doorway. "Hey, Sif," she murmured gently. "Know what I think? I think maybe Loki likes you, has a feeling you like Thor, and made fun of Thor because he's jealous."

Sif made a goofy face at her. "Enough with all the *liking*, Ms. Girlgoddess of Love. And anyway, if Loki liked me, why would he mess up my tiles?"

"To get your attention? Who knows why boys do what they do?" said Freya. She started to leave again, then added, "Hey, let's all four of us sit together at dinner when Skade gets back, okay?"

"Sure!" Sif smiled, pleased at the invitation, since the podmates didn't always eat together. Odin's list of school rules, which he'd passed out last week, included not sitting with the exact same group for more than one meal a day. All part of his plan to promote increased mingling among students to help different worlds get along better. However, the Thunder Girls hadn't eaten together since the previous night.

After Freya and Idun were gone, Sif decided to go find Loki and give him a big fat piece of her mind. It was a mean trick he'd played on poor Idun, shape-shifting into an eagle and stealing one of her special apples. But first Sif undid her looped braids and combed out her long golden hair. After gathering it into a loose ponytail, she knotted it at the back of her head. Ah, that was better! More *her*. She grabbed her wool cloak from the back of the door, then quickly left Vingolf.

3
Boygods

As soon as Sif was outside the girls' dorm, she tried to think where to start her search for Loki. Though it had stopped snowing, a fierce wind was blowing. Having forgotten to take her mittens and not wanting to go to all the trouble of removing her boots again in order to get them, Sif blew on her hands to warm them as she stood awhile, thinking.

That mischievous boygod could be almost anywhere. After he'd finished his stolen apple, he might have gone to Breidablik Hall, the dorm where the boys lived. Or he might have kept his eagle form and flown off in search of someone else to annoy. Making up her mind, she started toward Breidablik.

Luckily, the two dorms weren't far apart. After passing the Valhallateria, she spotted Breidablik's copper roof gleaming in the weak sunlight that shone through the clouds. In minutes she was at the front door. From within she could hear someone playing a lute, a stringed instrument with a deep, round back. She knocked, and seconds later the door opened.

A boy with curly brown hair stood in the entryway. His name was Bragi. He was the boygod of poetry, and since he was holding a lute in one hand, she guessed he was the one who'd been playing.

"I'm looking for Loki," said Sif, going on tiptoe to peer around Bragi. The dorm's inner door was propped open, and through it she could see that the boys' common area looked much the same as the girls', except messier. She'd heard that this hall had eighteen sleeping pods, just like the girls' hall did. She could see a few boys running around inside and laughing, but none were Loki.

Bragi shook his curly head. "Haven't seen him."

"Could you check his sleeping pod?" Sif persisted hopefully. Girls weren't allowed beyond the communal room in the boys' hall (and vice versa with boys in the girls' hall), so it wasn't like she could go check for herself.

Shaking his head again, Bragi said, "Nope. He's one of my podmates, and I just came from our room, so I'd know if he was there."

"Any clue where he might be?" she asked.

Bragi creased his brow, as if thinking. Then he raised his lute and began to strum its strings. "Where Loki goes, nobody knows," the god of poetry sang out. "But if I were thee, I'd check the V."

"Uh, thanks for the tip, guess I'll make that trip," said Sif, grinning as she rhymed back at him. She turned and backtracked to the Valhallateria. Along the way she kept her eyes peeled for eagles flying beneath Yggdrasil's leafy canopy or perching in the smaller trees that grew atop Yggdrasil's huge branches. She didn't see any, though.

Just as the V's sparkling gold-thatched roof came into view, a girl with long, wavy black hair that had thick streaks of white in it came toward her. "Hey, Sif!" her podmate called. "Look at these cool new boots I bought at Midgard Mall!" Skade's cheeks were red from the cold, and she was wearing a white faux-fur hat with flaps that covered her ears.

Sif looked down at Skade's feet as the girls met up. "Snazzy," she said, admiring the sparkly red boots. "Since you already have a blue pair, you only need a green pair to match all three colors of the Bifrost Bridge." That was the tricolor rainbow bridge that ran from Asgard (located on the top ring), all the way down to Midgard (a world on the second ring). Its colors represented fire

43

(red), air (blue), and water (green). The Aesir, which was what the goddesses and gods of Asgard were called, had built the bridge.

Though Sif had only been teasing about the green boots, an interested light came into Skade's eyes. Sif had a feeling there would be a new pair of green boots in this girlgoddess's future. Skade pulled off one of her new boots and, while hopping on one leg, showed Sif the boot's thick fleece lining. "These'll be perfect for winter, see? And I got them for a super-great price on sale." She cocked her head at Sif. "Hey, that sale's still on. Maybe you should look for new boots too!"

"Thanks, but I'm good," Sif told her. She had just two pairs: the pair of plain, sturdy black ones that she was currently wearing, and a pair of fancy, fun white ones. That was plenty. She had only two feet, after all! "Hey, you haven't seen Loki around, have you?"

Skade slipped her boot back on. "No, why?"

Sif explained what had happened to Idun. "Freya

and I are pretty sure that eagle was Loki in disguise," she concluded.

"Wouldn't put it past him," Skade said, scowling. "I haven't seen him, though. Or an eagle, either." Soon the girls parted, saying they'd meet up again in a few minutes at dinner.

Sif was almost to the V when she heard Thor in the distance behind her. "Whoa! WHOA!" he boomed out. Sounded like he was headed her way. Who was he talking to?

Recalling Freya's Sif-Thor crushing theory, Sif panicked. Reluctant to face him while still thinking about that embarrassing stuff, she backed into a thicket at the side of the branchway. Using her (not-so-great) shape-shifting skills, she transformed into a rowan tree. It was one of only two forms she could take, the other being a swan. A swan would have stuck out too much, she figured, while a tree would blend in with Yggdrasil's leafy branches.

No sooner had she transformed than Thor came into sight. He was driving his chariot, which was drawn by his two goats, Tanngrisnir ("teeth barer") and Tanngnjóstr ("teeth grinder"). Since most chariots were drawn by horses, he got teased about these goats plenty, and not just by Loki. But Thor always laughed it off, saying his goats were better at the job. In Sif's opinion, this showed he had a good sense of humor.

"Whoa!" Thor yelled again. His chariot was careening wildly, lurching from side to side as it came down the branchway toward Sif. Something must've spooked his goats! The red-haired boygod's attempts to halt them were to no avail. At the last moment the chariot swerved toward the thicket of branches where she had hidden. Oh no!

As he passed, Thor reached out and grabbed hold of one of Sif's branches with both his hands. "Ow!" she yelped, for the branch was actually a long lock of her hair, magically disguised. But he couldn't know that.

Luckily, Thor didn't hear her over the commotion. He was too busy using her hair . . . um . . . *branch* to swing himself free of the chariot. When his two goats swerved to the other side of the branchway, he let go of Sif and dropped safely to the ground. The goats broke free of their harnesses and raced off, while the chariot skidded to a stop on its side.

Still in her rowan form, Sif watched Thor run after his two goats and corral them. As he was bringing them back to the chariot, Loki appeared out of nowhere. "What happened?" he asked, surveying the scene.

Thor scratched his head. "Tanngrisnir and Tanngnjóstr just bolted all of a sudden. You okay, guys?" Petting the goats, he bent and began to check them over for injuries.

Loki shook his head. "Gosh, I wonder what could've caused them to take off like that?"

Thor was so busy with his goats that he didn't notice the mischievous glint in Loki's eyes or the smile that was playing around his lips. Sif did, though. It was a total tip-off. She was sure Loki had done something to make those goats stampede! He'd probably shape-shifted into a mouse or some other small creature and darted between the goats' hooves, making them startle. Most likely to get back at Thor for trying to punch him in Runes class earlier.

Sif rustled her branches in indignation. Unfortunately, Loki's keen eye caught the movement. "Hmm," he said, frowning at her leafy arms. "What is a rowan tree doing growing in Yggdrasil's branches?"

Uh-oh. During the very first week of school, Loki, who could transform himself into virtually anything, had wasted no time in teasing her about her limited shape-shifting skills when she had made the mistake of mentioning them. Sif held very still now trying not to give herself away.

"I don't know, but it's a good thing it was there," Thor replied. "When I thought my chariot was going to crash, I caught one of that rowan's branches and swung out a few seconds before my goats broke free. Saved me from nine worlds of hurt!" Seeming satisfied that his goats were okay, he crouched to examine his chariot. His muscles flexed and bunched as he pushed it upright onto its wheels again.

Loki's dark-blue eyes were sparkling as he studied rowan-Sif. "Hmm, who do I know that can shape-shift into a rowan tree?" he asked, tapping his chin with one finger. Then suddenly he lunged across the path and caught hold of one of her branches. Her arm, this time.

"Ow!" she yelled as he yanked it.

"Ha! I knew it," crowed Loki, hearing her. She tried to shake her branch-arm free of his grip, but he just grinned and held on tighter. "Come out, Sif! I know you're in there. Unshift!"

Upon his words, Sif felt herself begin to change back to her girlgoddess form. Because if someone caught hold of you while you were in shape-shift mode and commanded you to unshift, you couldn't prevent yourself from doing so. That was simply how shape-shifting magic worked.

As she took her goddess form again, Loki found himself holding her arm instead of a branch. He laughed. "Gotcha!"

"You . . . you . . . *bonehead*!" she yelled at him, jerking away and rubbing her arm. Thor, who'd been rotating his chariot's wheels to check their balance, looked over his shoulder and blinked at her in surprise.

"Question is, why were you hiding?" Loki asked her. His gaze went to Thor, then came back to her. Then he grinned.

Before he could leap to any embarrassing conclusions, especially in front of Thor, Sif huffed, "If I want to branch out, that's my business."

Loki smirked snidely.

This only made Sif angrier at him, and her hands fisted at her sides. "You'd better watch it, Loki. Freya and I are onto you, you Idun-scaring eagle. And if we even *sense* that you're giving her any more trouble, we'll go straight to Odin." Though this wasn't something she and Freya had actually discussed doing, she felt certain Freya would agree to it.

Loki shot her an intrigued look. "Sense? Are you hinting that you can foresee things?"

Ignoring his question, Sif took a step forward and stuck her face up in his face. "I *sense* that you caused Thor's 'accident' just now. Am I right?"

Still crouched next to his chariot, Thor must have been listening to them. Because now his eyes narrowed as he swung around to glare at Loki.

But Loki was still focused on Sif. "Ooh, I'm sooo scared of Sif the Great Seer who can sense everything I do!" Making his eyes comically large and round, he drew back a step. Then, with his palms facing toward her, he wiggled his fingers as if in fright.

Thor jumped to his feet. "Leaf—I mean, LEAVE her alone!" he yelled at Loki.

Loki just laughed again, ignoring him. "First of all, you can't prove a thing," he said to Sif. "Second, your puny prophesying skills are just sad. And third, you have a weird braid in your hair." He reached around her and tugged on a braid she'd unknowingly missed in her long golden ponytail.

"Ow!" she cried, pulling away. After tugging the band out of her ponytail, she located the remaining braid and started undoing it.

"Guess you didn't foresee *that* coming," Loki said smugly. "I doubt you could predict the future even if it was staring you right in the face."

Thor balled his hands into fists and advanced on Loki a couple of steps. "I TOLD YOU TO BACK OFF!" he boomed in a voice so loud, it could probably be heard in the third-ring world of the dead, clear down in Niflheim.

Oh great, thought Sif as she banded her now braid-free hair back into a ponytail. This was getting sooo ridiculous! "It's okay, Thor. I can handle this."

"But . . . you sure?" Thor started to protest.

Loki grinned at him. "You heard what she said, goat boy. *Ba-a-ack* off." He was obviously mocking the way Thor's goats bleated, trying to rile the boy even more. And it worked.

The superstrong boygod's face turned redder than his hair. Angry on his behalf as well as her own, Sif lashed out. "For your information, Loki, I can too predict the future. And I can prove it!"

Instantly she clapped her hand over her mouth and wished she could take the words back. Telling Freya that she was (sort of) a seer was one thing, but *Loki*? How dumb could she be?

Sif braced herself for his reaction. She was astonished to see a look of fear flit across the boy's face. Was he scared of seers? Maybe he didn't have that power himself and was worried she'd be able to guess his mischief-making plans and get him into trouble?

But then the look of fear was gone, leaving her to wonder if she'd only imagined it.

"Sure you are," he said with a sneer. (Which was the kind of reaction she'd expected all along!)

"It's true," she insisted, hoping he really was afraid of seers. She put her hands on her hips. "In fact, I fore-saw that you would steal Freya's necklace!" For better or worse, her secret was definitely out now.

But Loki only rolled his eyes. "Humph! Doubt it. It's easy to predict events that have already happened. Even a dummy like Thor could do that!"

Thor's big hands curled into fists again, and his eyes shot daggers at Loki.

"Sorry. Just ki-i-idding, Thor!" Loki bleated out. "Ha-ha! I totally crack myself up sometimes!" He bent over, slapping his leg like his teasing was hilarious (which it definitely was not!).

Thor growled and made a grab for Loki. However, that wily boy was too fast. Thor's hands caught only air as Loki transformed into a grasshopper and quickly boinged away.

And suddenly Sif found herself hanging out alone with her not-a-crush. *Oh no!*

4
Thor

BLAST!" ROARED THOR. HE RUBBED THE back of his neck as grasshopper-Loki boinged off into the nearby forest. "I wasn't done yelling at him. If I'd been faster, I could have grabbed him and stopped him from transforming." He was referring to another rule of magic. It was impossible to shape-shift successfully if anyone else was *touching* you.

Sif nodded. "That would've been a *hoppy* thing, because that guy really *bugs* me sometimes," she said, joking nervously. (She was okay talking to boys, but she wasn't sure how to talk to a maybe-or-not-crush!)

Thor chuckled at her teeny jokes, which was nice of him, because she knew they were kind of lame. Afterward there was a silent, awkward pause. Thor shifted from one big foot to the other and tucked his thumbs in the top of his Belt-o'-Power. Was he as nervous trying to talk to her as she was to him? "Well . . . ," she began, starting to sidle away.

Suddenly Sif felt a nudge on her arm. Tanngrisnir, who was slightly smaller than Tanngnjóstr, though they were both the same gray color, had trotted up and butted her gently with his horned head. (Saved by the goat!)

"Hey, stop that," Thor scolded him.

"It's okay." She reached down and scratched the goat between his horns. "You just want attention, right, sweetie?"

Thor smiled at her as Tanngnjóstr wandered over to him to be petted too. "Yeah. Maybe I should change

Tanngrisnir's name to Loki. He can't stand not being the center of attention either. That guy is such a pain." He frowned.

"So where were you coming from in your chariot, anyway?" Sif asked, changing the subject so Thor wouldn't keep thinking about Loki. (Otherwise, he might decide to go after him again!) She moved her fingers to scratch Tanngrisnir behind one ear.

"I was on my way back from guard duty," Thor replied as he ran a hand along Tanngnjóstr's back. "A bunch of us were out patrolling the border wall."

"Any problems?" she asked. All students took turns doing guard duty. Sif's last shift had been yesterday.

Thor nodded. "Yeah, I spotted two frost giants trying to tunnel under it. We all hoped that new wall would discourage attacks on Asgard. But instead those giants seem more determined than ever. It's like they enjoy the challenge!" Then he grinned. "Anyway, they got stuck, so we just wound up helping them get loose.

Heimdall gave 'em a lecture and sent them running home to Jotunheim." Jotunheim, the world of the frost giants, was on the second ring, alongside the world of Midgard, where humans lived.

Sif laughed. She couldn't help thinking how much Loki, a half-giant like Skade, enjoyed a challenge too. Only, his challenges usually involved teasing and playing tricks on other students, while Skade's challenges involved skiing steep, snowy mountains and discovering boot sales!

It was a few seconds before Sif realized that silence had fallen between her and Thor again. Her cheeks warmed as she stopped petting Tanngrisnir and straightened. "Okay . . . um . . . I guess I'll . . . see you later?" Abruptly she turned and hurried toward the Valhallateria. Though the horn signaling the dinner hour had yet to sound, her podmates might be inside already.

"Wait up!" Thor called to her. Quickly he tethered

his goats to his chariot again, hopped in, and then rolled over to ride alongside her. "So are you really a seer, then?"

At her somewhat reluctant nod he went on, "How does it work? Can you do it without using runes? And can you foresee *everything* that's going to happen?"

"No way. Just a few things every now and then," she replied in answer to his last question. "And yes, I can do it without runes." She hoped he wasn't going to ask her what she saw in his future, like some kids at her old school used to do before the Horrible Thing happened with her then best friend. After that she'd clammed up about her abilities and claimed she had never really had them.

"I wish *I* was good at seeing the future," Thor told her. "I'd stop Loki from making trouble before he does it!"

"Be careful what you wish for," she replied. She wasn't exactly sure yet how she felt about others knowing she could see. In one way, it was kind of a relief that her secret was out, even if some, like Loki, might not believe her. Denying and hiding her talent all these years had taken a lot of effort.

When they reached the Valhallateria, Thor leaped down from his chariot and tied it and his goats to a gold ring stuck in a grassy patch of ground to the left of the V's doors. The grass could thrive in snow and had been planted here and elsewhere to keep forest animals from nibbling on Yggdrasil too much. There was even a dragon named Nidhogg down on the third world ring that liked to gnaw at the ginormous tree's roots!

Yggdrasil faced all kinds of threats, and not just from animals that liked to snack on it. The war between Asgard and Vanaheim, as well as lesser battles, had a bad effect on the World Tree over time, causing it and the plants that grew upon its enormous branches to droop. Since Yggdrasil sheltered all nine worlds, the survival of everyone and everything was dependent on keeping the tree healthy!

As soon as his chariot and goats were secured, Thor grabbed one of the Valhallateria's V-shaped handles and pulled the door open wide. "After you," he said gallantly. Then he stepped aside to let Sif pass.

"Thanks," she murmured. Thor was full of surprises. She hadn't known this rough, tough, superstrong guy could also be so polite!

Inside, Sif glanced around for her podmates, but they weren't there yet. Only a few students were at the tables so far, seated in chairs that had wooden shields as seats and backs, and bent spears for legs. Thor continued to hold the door open for some other students after Sif had passed through. So she walked on a few steps without him, thinking she might go grab something to drink and wait for her friends. Then she saw something that made her freeze in her tracks.

Oh no! The one girl she really, really did not want to see was sitting at a table close by. The girl's back was to her, but Sif would have recognized that black, short-cropped hair anywhere. It was Lofn—her used-to-be best friend! The one she'd done the nearly tragic Horrible Thing to back in second grade. Familiar guilt over the memory filled her.

The two of them had been the only ones chosen from their village to attend Asgard Academy. Fortunately, they didn't often run into each other. It helped that they had no classes together. And also that Lofn tended to hang out in her sleeping pod more than in the common area of Vingolf Hall. Sif had a feeling they were both making an effort to avoid each other.

Suddenly Lofn's head turned. *Yikes!* Sif sped off before their gazes could connect, heading for Heidrun, the big ceramic goat fountain that stood on a table in the middle of the dining hall. The apple juice that spurted into a trough from the fountain's many spigots was made from the special gold-colored apples that Idun collected. The ones that kept all the goddesses and gods youthful.

Apparently done with his self-assigned door-holding

duties, Thor came over to the goat fountain now too. The table it stood upon had a pedestal shaped like a stout tree trunk and green-painted leaves that formed a flat, rectangular top. Rows of drinking horns and short, green, round-bottomed cups called *hrimkalders* were stacked on the tabletop among its green-painted leaves. She and Thor took *hrimkalders* and began to fill them from Heidrun's spigots.

As Sif waited for her cup to fill, her eyes automatically flicked to the big red emergency button that was encased in a glass dome on a wooden column behind the table. The button was labeled:

X540

Push only

in the event

of Ragnarok

Like the Horrible Thing involving Lofn, Ragnarok was something she preferred not to think about. In

Ragnarok Survival Skills class they'd learned that it was a terrible event that would happen sometime in the future, leading to the destruction of all nine worlds! As for the significance of the number 540, none of the students knew what it meant, and none dared break the glass and press the button to find out. Not even Loki!

When both of their cups were full, Sif gave Thor a quick nod and then headed for a table far from Lofn to wait for her podmates. Once she was seated, she glanced toward the fountain again. Thor was still standing near it looking around for his friends, who hadn't arrived yet either. His eyes flicked toward her and, once again, their eyes caught.

"Crushes often start with just looking," Freya had said. *Scratch that*, thought Sif. This was *not* a crush, not yet at least. But couldn't *friendship* start with just looking too?

Thor appeared a little lost standing there. It seemed dumb, not to mention mean, to ignore him, so she waved him over. Because it was the polite thing to do. When he drew near, she said, "Want to sit with me till our friends get here?"

"Yeah, sure," he said, sounding pleased. He plopped into a chair across the table from her, and they sat silently sipping their drinks for about a minute. Then he jumped in with, "Hey, thanks for . . . um . . . the save back there with my chariot. It was cool of you to go *out on a limb* for me." His eyes twinkled at her.

Sif grinned at his joke about her rowan transformation. "Yeah, well, glad I could help. I could see you were *shaking like a leaf* there for a second."

At this, Thor laughed, his voice booming across the V and turning some heads. Yes, this boygod was big and often loud. And he sometimes lost his temper and was too quick to want to fight. But now she saw that he could also be good-natured, with the same kind of goofy humor she had.

It was nice of him to thank her, even though she

hadn't exactly *intended* to rescue him. That had been a lucky accident—unlike the accident itself, which she was sure had been intentional. That Loki!

Just then a group of Valkyries appeared from the kitchen. Those muscular cafeteria ladies all wore gleaming metal helmets with tall wings on either side and carved *V*s in front. Across their chests they wore breastplates with rows of loops down the front that held silver spoons and knives and fresh rolled-up napkins. Each Valkyrie carried a six-foot-wide tray loaded with many steaming bowls of food, as well as baskets of bread and cheese—all balanced on one hand.

"Everyone, take a seat! It's time to eat!" the armor-clad servers sang out in loud, operatic voices. (*Hmm. Did Bragi write that rhyming song for them?* Sif wondered. *Could be!*)

Whoosh! Large wings sprouted from the Valkyries' backs, causing them to lift off a foot or so above the ground. They flew in different directions to pass out the food and cutlery. Momentarily distracted by them, Sif and Thor watched as they set places at tables and handed out bowls of lamb and cabbage stew with military efficiency.

The dining hall had begun to fill with students, but neither Sif's nor Thor's podmates had arrived yet. So they kept sitting together. Tearing his eyes away from the cafeteria ladies and the delicious-smelling stew they were handing around, Thor leaned across the table toward Sif. "So what was your runeword in class today? You didn't get called on, and I was wondering."

She shrugged. *"Mjollnir."*

"Any idea what it foretold? Since you can see the future, whatever you saw in your runeword would come true, right?" His eyes gleamed with interest. Why hadn't she noticed their striking color until now? They were the blue of a glacier lit by sunshine! There was an intelligence behind those eyes that put the lie to Loki's "dummy" taunt. Loki had called Thor *ugly*, too. Sif

68

wished she could tell him that he wasn't dumb *or* ugly. But that might give him the wrong idea about how she felt about him.

"I guess it could mean that we're going to be getting some new tool or method for crushing enemy giants. Because, you know, the definition of *mjollnir* is—"

"'To crush,'" Thor supplied. As if to illustrate, he pounded one fist into the palm of his other hand.

Thank goodness that other meaning of the word "crush"—the liking meaning that Freya had mentioned—didn't occur to him!

"What do you think the new tool or method will be?" he asked eagerly.

Before she could tell him that this information hadn't revealed itself to her (not yet, anyway), the dishes and cutlery on other tables around them began to rattle so hard that some fell to the floor. The tables lurched back and forth, and a low thumping sound reached everyone's ears.

She and Thor leaped to their feet, eyes rounding

big. "What's happening?" Sif wondered aloud.

"Earthquake!" someone yelled from across the room.

"No! *Giant*quake!" Thor yelled back. The expression on his face was grim as he glanced at Sif and murmured, "Same thing happened while I was on guard duty today. Frost giants were holding marching drills in the mountains."

Sif gasped. "This sounds a lot closer than that."

"Yeah. They're getting more daring. Something's up," said Thor. "I'd better go check with Odin. See if he wants some of us doing double guard duty." Before Sif could even say good-bye, he was across the room in a few quick strides. He lifted one of the bowls of stew from a Valkyrie's tray and took it with him, exiting the V minutes before Freya, Skade, and Idun entered.

The three girls raced over to Sif. "Did you feel that rocking and rolling just now?" Freya asked as she, Idun, and Skade sat down around Sif's table.

"Yeah!" said Sif, dropping back into her own seat. "Thor said it was caused by *giants*!"

Skade, who was of course a half-giant, groaned and rolled her eyes. "Ugh. Sometimes my relatives are sooo embarrassing! Always making trouble."

Clank! Clank! Clank! Clank! An efficient Valkyrie had reached their table and plunked down four bowls of stew and cutlery, then zoomed off before the girls could thank her.

As the four girlgoddesses dug into their food, Freya went on. "We passed Thor on the way in and, um, Ratatosk was telling him some . . . stuff."

Sif noticed her three friends share a worried look. Ratatosk was an extra-large squirrel that loved to spread gossip to stir up trouble. He continually ran up and down Yggdrasil's trunk, branches, and roots carrying news from the tip-top of the tree, where an eagle sat, to the very bottom of the third ring, where Nidhogg the root-nibbling dragon lurked.

"What stuff?" asked Sif between bites of her lamb and cabbage stew. *Mmm. Delicious.*

"Seems there are reports from Midgard," Idun informed her. "Reports saying the giants have been sneaking into farmers' fields at night and cutting down wheat to stockpile it for their troops."

"What? No!" Sif said in dismay. Those crops fed all nine worlds. She hadn't ever mentioned it to her podmates, but it was her job to watch over them. Her golden hair's magic was what protected the wheat and made it grow abundantly! "That's not fair. The wheat is to be shared. We have to stop them!" She looked around wildly, unsure what to do.

Idun frowned. "Giants must grow wheat of their own in Jotunheim, though. So why would they need Midgard's wheat too?"

"Good question," said Freya, dipping a piece of bread in her stew. The girls all looked at Skade. As a half-giant, she ought to know the answer.

Skade swallowed a big bite of bread and cheese, then said, "Sure, plenty of wheat grows in Jotunheim. So,

72

though it hurts me to say this, being half-giant myself, I have to wonder if this wheat-stealing could be part of some bigger plot."

"If that were true, wouldn't your family tell you, or some of the girlgiants here at AA?" asked Freya.

Skade let out a sigh. "Not necessarily. We giants can be a sneaky bunch. Information is often on a need-to-know basis." She turned to Sif. "Speaking of sneaky, I wonder if Loki knows anything about all this. Did you ever catch up to him?"

"Mm-hmm." A glance around the V told Sif that he hadn't yet shown up. Quickly she told her podmates about Thor almost crashing and how she suspected Loki had been the cause. She edited the story a little, however, leaving out her transformation into a rowan tree and Loki's teasing.

Idun sighed. "That Loki. I hate to speak badly of anyone, but . . ."

"But people like Loki kind of deserve to be spoken

badly of," Skade finished, sounding like she was only half joking. "He should be punished for the mean things he does, but he always seems to get away with them. Wish someone could spy on him all the time. Then we'd have proof he's making trouble, no matter what shape he takes."

Idun turned toward Sif and Freya. "Hey, you guys are seers. Can't you see what he's up to when he's not around? Spy on him, in other words?"

"Huh? How did you . . . ," Sif started to ask. Then she shot Freya a look. Her podmate shrugged apologetically, giving Sif her answer. But really, Sif had never asked her not to tell anyone about her secret talent. For all she knew, *Lofn* had already told her podmates about the trouble Sif's prophesying had caused her years ago, though no word of this had reached Sif's ears.

While she was pondering this, Freya grinned at Idun and said, "No, seeing doesn't work like that. So please don't ask us to tell you your future. It's not that easy."

Skade waved her spoon and laughed. "I'm not sure I'd *want* to know mine anyway. Could be trouble!"

Sif had a feeling her friends were joking around a bit to ease her stress about the wheat. It was helping. A little.

"Uh-oh. Speaking of trouble," she murmured. She lifted her chin to indicate one of the carved wooden friezes that hung near the girls' table. These painted friezes covered all of the V's walls and were peopled with heroic warriors who had died in battle. The warriors had been brought into the friezes by Odin's Valkyries as painted figures that magically came to life toward the end of every meal. When they did, it was not a good idea to stick around.

As all four girls studied the nearby frieze, an armor-clad warrior reached out of it to grab a dish of lemon-flavored snow pudding from a Valkyrie rushing by with a tray of the desserts. With a wide grin on his face, the warrior took aim and then flung the snow pudding at a painting of heroes directly across the room. The girls' table was directly in its path!

"Incoming!" yelled Skade. The four girls ducked just in time. The pudding sailed over their heads to hit the painting beyond them. *Splat!*

Calls of "Food fight!" "Run!" "Flee the V!" went up from AA students. They leaped up and headed for the exit doors.

Meanwhile, whoops and hollers rang out from the friezes as apples, turnips, potatoes, and other food flew back and forth across the room. *Thunk! Sploosh!* Most was directed at warriors occupying friezes on opposite walls, but occasionally the thrown food accidentally hit students, too!

"Time to go!" Freya yelled, though no one needed to be told that. Sif and the other girls were already scrambling from their seats. Phew! These end-of-meal food fights were a constant at the V. They were funny, but they could also get really messy!

The food fight had taken their minds off their real troubles for the moment. However, as soon as the four girls were outside, the branchway rolled under their feet causing them to wobble and stumble on the path. Overhead, Yggdrasil's branches groaned and shook.

"Another giantquake!" yelped Sif.

As the girls tried to stay upright, Freya called over to her, "Have you tried to foresee what those giants are up to?" When Sif shook her head no, Freya added, "I tried, but I wasn't able to. I've got a bad feeling about all this." The rolling stopped abruptly, making her next words sound loud in the sudden quiet. "A Ragnarok kind of feeling."

Sif and the others gasped in shock. "You think the frost giants might be trying to start Ragnarok . . . now?" asked Idun. They'd always been told that the end of the world was an event that would take place in the faraway future!

"Who knows how it'll start, or when? We'd better . . . ,"

said Freya. Then, something seemed to occur to her. "Rats! Just remembered I have a pet party scheduled in the dorm just minutes from now to showcase some of the jewelry I've been making especially for pets. I'll cancel, though, so we can brainstorm what to do about all this."

"Wait!" said Skade. "I heard a bunch of the girl-giants say they're going to that party. I'll come too. Maybe I can get them to accidentally spill any secret information they might have about a giant plot. Idun, you're good at reading people. Can you come too?"

"Sure," Idun agreed.

Sif nodded. "Good plan. While you're doing that, I'll go to the library. I can look up information about Ragnarok and find out what events are supposed to lead up to it. Hopefully not giants stealing wheat crops! And maybe I'll research the art of seeing, too, in case anything helpful leaps out at me. The more we know the better, because . . ."

The four girls finished her sentence as one, exclaiming, "Knowledge is power!" They bumped elbows and laughed, briefly easing the tension. This was the school's motto, spelled out in runes above the Heartwood Library door.

After their giggles died away, Sif split off from the other girls to go in a different direction, Sif to the library and the other three girlgoddesses to Vingolf Hall.

As Sif headed off down the snowy path alone, her mood was lighter than it might have been if she and her podmates hadn't brainstormed a plan to find out more about the frost giant problem. And by working together, it seemed like they were on their way to becoming true friends. This wasn't something she'd foreseen, just something she felt in her hopeful heart.

Unfortunately, her prophetic powers had failed to alert her to the beady-eyed bird that had been perched directly above her and her podmates on one of Yggdrasil's branches. As the girls had been talking, that cunning magpie had taken in everything they'd said.

5
The Heartwood Library

Aꜰᴛᴇʀ ꜱʜᴇ ᴘᴀʀᴛᴇᴅ ꜰʀᴏᴍ ʜᴇʀ ᴛʜʀᴇᴇ podmates, Sif made her way through a golden forest to the Heartwood Library (so named because it was located at the very center—the *heart*—of Yggdrasil's tree trunk). Its existence had once been hidden, but Freya had uncovered it just after coming to Asgard Academy.

To enter Yggdrasil's trunk, Sif used her fingertip to trace the words "Knowledge is power" on her palm. These were the very words she and the other girls had just giggled over, of course. After she finished palm-tracing, she stepped forward to stand nose-and-toes to tree bark. Instantly she found herself transported inside the trunk, all the way to the hollowed-out center of the enormous World Tree. It took powerful magic to do something like that. *Yggdrasil* magic!

Thump! Sif landed standing on a round wooden floor about two hundred feet across with a large hole at its center. The Heartwood Library was such an amazing place that she couldn't resist taking a few moments to gaze around in wonder, as she always did.

Through the hole she could see many other floors with similar holes descending beneath the floor she'd landed on. Several transparent tubular slides with diameters ranging from one to four feet corkscrewed up to her current level through holes from somewhere far below. On the day Freya had discovered this place, she had corkscrewed her way through one of the slides all the way down to the second world ring!

Yggdrasil's curved inner walls were lined with runebook-filled shelves that extended from floor to floor as far downward as Sif could see. There were ladders on wheels that followed tracks here and there along the shelves. By climbing from one ladder to another, you could easily reach all the other floors and their books. And scattered throughout the library on every floor were comfy seating areas.

Suddenly a column of bright-blue water shot through one of the tubular slides to bubble up in a tall, fountain-like spout at eye level. Atop the spout sat a disembodied bald head! *Glub, glub.* "May I help you?" the head asked her pleasantly.

This was Mimir, who was quite literally the *head* librarian. In other words, he had a head but no attached body! Freya had discovered him here. He had been hiding out in the library ever since the Asgard-Vanaheim war began, while protecting Asgard's gold from giants.

Since Sif could see the section on Ragnarok from

where she stood, she only said, "I'm looking for information on prophesying."

Before she could continue, Mimir's head twirled around once in excitement. When it stopped, a smile brightened his face. "My favorite subject!"

He had lost his body around the start of the Asgard-Vanaheim war. Good thing his head seemed to work just fine without it. In addition to being incredibly smart, he was an oracle known in all nine worlds for the accuracy and power of his prophecies. In fact, Odin often consulted him.

"You'll want the Future Studies section," Mimir told her. "Next floor down and to the right of the direction you're now facing." Cocking his head, he added, "I have a meeting with Odin at the Well of Urd in a moment and may be gone for an hour or so."

"Okay," said Sif. "Thanks for your help."

But he hardly noticed her reply, for he was already yelling, "Gullveig! Where's that gift from Ms. Frigg?"

At his summons the library assistant came over. She was wearing tons of gold chains and smiled at Sif as she set an orange-and-white waterproof cap on top of Mimir's head. Then she tied its dangling straps under his chin. The cap had a ruffle attached to its top front edge, making it resemble a baby bonnet. Hey! It looked like the thing Ms. Frigg had been knitting in Runes class. So it must've been intended as a gift for Mimir. As usual, her knitted creations proved giggle-worthy.

"Gullveig is off work in another few minutes," Mimir told Sif, directing a kind smile at his assistant. "But if you should need me, just push this switch over to the right and I'll immediately pop back up." Here he glanced meaningfully at a green-colored switch that sat beside him at the top of the slide. It must be the switch that reversed the direction of the water flow, Sif realized.

"Ready?" Gullveig asked Mimir.

The librarian bobbed his head. His assistant's gold chains swung forward as she reached down and pushed the green switch over to the left. The water, which had been flowing upward to keep Mimir balanced at the top of the slide, immediately reversed itself. Caught in the downward flow, Mimir shouted "Whee!" as he whirled through the maze of transparent tubular slides, descending from floor to floor and eventually disappearing from view.

Gullveig grinned and winked at Sif. Speaking fondly of Mimir, she said, "Smarter than anyone, but goofy as a happy little kid when it comes to those slides."

"How will he get back up?" Sif asked curiously.

"Nose nudge," Gullveig informed her. "There are more switches in various places and at the bottom of the tree. He can push them with his nose if no one's around to help."

After Gullveig left, Sif quickly went to the Ragnarok section and found a list of happenings that were supposed to lead up to that terrible event.

Ragnarok would take place in winter. One of the first things to herald it would be warnings from three roosters. A blast from Heimdall's horn would bring the dead heroes out of the friezes and back to life, and then a great battle would take place in the Valhallateria! Wow, talk about a major food fight!

Ragnarok would mean much more, as she already knew from Ragnarok Survival Skills class. In the end, all nine worlds would be destroyed. Yggdrasil, too. Sif shuddered at the idea. At least now she knew what incidents would hint to them that it was beginning.

Hmm. It was already winter. Still, she hadn't heard any roosters crowing so far, thank goodness!

Deciding she'd learned enough, she used the ladders to go down one floor, where she easily located the Future Studies section. As far as she could tell, she was the only student in the library right now. On a Friday evening, others would likely be skiing, skating, or sledding, hanging out in Breidablik or Vingolf, or on guard duty. When she reached the section labeled FUTURE STUDIES, she began to browse the runebooks on the shelves.

Because of her reading difficulties, sometimes even deciphering runebooks' titles took time and effort. Sif ran a finger down each book's spine, pausing as necessary to wait for the rune-letters to stop shifting around. Among the titles were *Prophesying for Dummies*, *How to Win Friends and Influence the Future*, *See Tomorrow Today*, and *The Rudiments of Rune Spells*.

That last title stopped her cold. Runes had been the cause of the Horrible Thing! Still, using runes to see into the future might help her figure out what those frost giants were up to, stealing and stockpiling wheat crops. If only she could figure out some way to guarantee there would never be a problem like the one she'd caused Lofn if she started prophesying again . . .

"Maybe instead of avoiding you, I should learn everything about you," she murmured, tapping her fingertip on the word "rune" on the book's spine. "If there's a way I can use you to safely prophesy, without causing another Horrible Thing to happen, I want to know."

She took down the runebook and carried it to a nearby table. It was warm in the library, so she slipped off her cloak and draped it over the comfy cushioned stool she'd pulled up to the table to sit on. Scanning the table of contents inside *The Rudiments of Rune Spells*, she saw from the chapter headings that the runebook contained mostly introductory stuff. ("What Are Runes?," "An Alphabet of Runes," "Why Are Runes Useful?," etc.) This was not unexpected, since "rudiments" was just a fancy word for "basic information."

She thumbed through the book, though, and sat up straighter when she came across something interesting in a later chapter. "'Difficult rune interpretations can sometimes be solved through dreams,'" she read aloud. "Now, this is more like it!"

The author of the book recommended repeating words that related to a particular runeword over and over in your mind as you went to sleep, but without making any effort at turning the runeword into a prophecy.

Supposedly, your brain would supply the connections to do that on its own through your dreams, which you'd recall when you woke up.

Hmm. Sif filed that information away. Then she skipped to the section on rune *writing*. "'Written runes carved into pieces of wood or stone as charms can be altered by certain persons under certain circumstances,'" she read. Well, thank goodness for that. Otherwise, what she'd done to Lofn could have turned out much, much worse than it had.

By this point *The Rudiments of Rune Spells*, which lacked many illustrations or diagrams, was getting kind of boring, and Sif caught herself yawning. Her sleepiness was made worse by the soothing sound of the water running through Mimir's tubular slides. *Bubble, bubble. Glub, glub.* Just one more chapter, she told herself as she struggled to keep her eyes open. But, oh, a nap would be so nice! Soon her head drooped onto her arms and she began to snooze. *Zzzz.*

Sometime later Sif woke with a start. She yawned, blinked, and looked around sleepily. For some reason she felt curiously lighter, and there was a cool breeze on her neck that she wasn't used to. She shivered. *Brr.* Time to go, she decided. She could come back another time to finish the research she'd started.

As she rose from her stool, her cloak slipped off of it and fell to the floor. She bent to pick up the cloak. And that's when she saw the soft, lustrous mass of long golden tresses heaped all around her stool.

Huh? In a panic, Sif flung her hands to her head. *"Arghhh!"* she screamed. Her hair, her beautiful hair. It had all been cut off!

No wonder she'd felt lighter. Gingerly she patted all around the top of her head. Her remaining hair was mere stubble now. No more than an inch long. She was a porcupine-head! Almost as bald as Mimir!

"Who would do such a cruel thing to me?" she wondered aloud. And not just to *her*, because this despicable act could have consequences for others, too. Without her hair—the source of her goddess powers—who knew what would happen to the golden fields of wheat that humans grew down in Midgard? Without her hair's magic, what would protect the grain and help it thrive?

Tears of anger (and embarrassment, too) began to fall from her eyes. She swung around, looking in every direction. "Who did this? Who cut my hair? Show yourself, you sneaky hair-snipper clipper!" she shouted. But no one appeared.

Wait a minute. *Clipper? Klippa! Loki!* His runeword in class that afternoon had been *klippa*—"to clip or cut." When she'd asked him what he thought it meant, he'd acted weird and claimed he didn't know.

"Liar!" she yelled into the empty library. His runeword had turned out to be prophetic, but it wouldn't surprise her if it was the word itself that had given Loki the idea to cut off her hair in the first place! Did he think this was funny or something? Well, it wasn't! And if cutting off her hair was an example of him trying to flirt with her, like Freya had speculated, this was totally the WRONG way to do it!

With tears streaming down her face, Sif gathered up the cut hair. Unfortunately, it had power only when it was growing on top of her head. Yet she knew of no magic spell that could reattach it. Sadly, it was no good to her anymore. Or to anyone else, for that matter. So she found a pretty wooden box and lovingly placed her tresses inside, then set the box in the trash can.

"Farewell, fair hair," she said over it, as if she were at a hair funeral and burying it in a grave.

Fury fueled her now as she wrapped herself in her cloak and flipped its hood over her practically bald head. "Knowledge is power," she murmured as she drew the words on her palm. Instantly she found herself outside Yggdrasil again. She scurried through the golden forest and down a branchway toward Vingolf Hall.

When the idea of making a wig floated into her

mind, she almost turned back for her hair. But even if she could successfully make one, it wouldn't lend her the same power as *growing* hair. Before she could decide, she heard footsteps pound behind her.

"Sif? Is that you? Wait up a minute!"

Recognizing the deep voice as Thor's, she felt her heart leap into her throat. She'd been hoping to get back to her room without meeting anyone. Thor was probably the very *last* person she wanted to see her right now! Not that people wouldn't find out about all this soon enough. Too bad hair grew so slowly. She wasn't aware of any magic that could make it grow faster.

Automatically Sif clasped the bottom edge of her hood with one hand, tightening it around her head. Pretending she hadn't heard Thor, she kept moving, almost jogging now. But with those long strides of his, the boy-god caught up to her anyway.

"Yep, turns out we do have a giant giant problem beyond our wall," he confided in a serious voice. "I'm not sure our weapons can keep them at bay. I can tell Odin's worried. The last thing he wants—the last thing *anyone* wants—is another war."

"Mm-hmm," Sif muttered. She didn't want to encourage him to go on. In addition to the wheat-stealing giants and that half-giant Loki, she had her *own* giant problem to worry about right now! She sped up.

"Well, I guess it's not really a new war," Thor corrected himself, easily keeping pace with her. "I mean, ever since the beginning of time, when Odin and his brothers slew the giant Ymir and built the nine worlds from his body, the frost giants have been fighting mad."

As everyone had learned in Norse History classes here at the academy or at their old schools, the sea had been formed from Ymir's sweat, mountains from his bones, trees from his hair, and the sky from his skull. The wall encircling the human world of Midgard had been made from Ymir's eyelashes, and from his brains clouds had been sculpted. Though all of this had happened in the far-distant past, frost giants had long memories.

Suddenly a puzzled expression came over Thor's face. "Wait, why are you being so quiet?" he asked, leaning around to try to see Sif's face deep within her hood. "You've hardly said a word the whole time we've been walking. Something wrong?"

"Um. Yes! I mean . . ." She gestured in frustration with both hands, releasing her grip on her hood. A brisk wind whipped up and her hood was blown back. *Oh no!* She caught it and flipped it back up to hide her semi-baldness. But it was too late. A shocked look entered Thor's glacier-blue eyes.

"That's . . . different," he murmured as they paused on the path to stare at each other. "Did you . . . um . . . cut it yourself? Is it the newest style or something?"

"What? No!" Sif exclaimed bitterly. "I'd *never* cut it. My hair is the source of my goddess powers!"

"Oh!" Thor's eyebrows shot up. "Yeah, so then why . . ." His brow furrowed.

"I didn't cut it!" she exploded, holding her hood more tightly closed as she spied other students coming toward them on the branchway. "I was asleep in the library and somebody else did."

Thor frowned suspiciously. "Loki?"

"Maybe. I mean, who else?" Sif replied mournfully. As they started off walking again, she explained about Loki's *klippa* runeword. "What did I ever do to him?" she went on fiercely, even as they turned up another branchway toward the dorms. "Nothing, that's what! Not that I know of, anyway." Carried away by her anger, she forgot for a minute who she was speaking to and added, "To do something like this—he must really hate me! Freya was totally wrong to think that he's been trying to flirt with me."

From the corner of her eye she watched Thor's jaw clamp tight. So did his fists. "Loki's reasons for doing anything are way too twisted to understand. But this time he's gone too far!" Seeming every bit as angry as her, he slammed a fist into the palm of his other hand and looked around, as if searching for Loki.

"Wait!" she warned. By now they had reached the entrance to Vingolf Hall. Facing Thor, she said firmly, "It's *my* hair and *my* magic. *I* want to handle this. I'm ninety-nine percent sure Loki was the one who cut it, but I want to talk to him before you clobber him or something. Maybe it was an accident or someone tricked him into it. Maybe he's sorry."

"He can say he's sorry all he wants, but this time Loki's going to *pay* for what he did!" Thor boomed.

"Loki does deserve to be punished, and I appreciate your wanting to help me," Sif told him earnestly. "Who knows how the loss of my hair will affect Midgard crops? You'll be adding to my worries if you try to punish Loki before I can question him, though. End of subject for now, okay?"

Thor shuffled his big feet for a moment or two, then reluctantly said, "'Kay."

"Thanks." With a quick wave, she started in through the hall's front door. In the mudroom she shucked off her boots and placed them in the racks. She tried not to cry again. Nothing but time could bring back her hair, she knew.

She clenched her teeth. It was bad enough that giants had been stealing Midgard's wheat. If what was left in the fields died, the consequences would be severe. Wheat was needed to make bread—a major source of food for humans. Without wheat, they might starve!

While thinking all this, Sif headed for the Thunder Girls' sleeping pod, ignoring anyone hanging about in the communal area and grasping her hood tight around her head. She was almost there when a horrible thought occurred to her. What if, when her hair regrew, it didn't have the same magical powers it had had before?

6
The Dream

WHEN SIF ENTERED THE SLEEPING POD, Freya, Skade, and Idun glanced up at her. They were playing some kind of card game together, sitting cross-legged on one of the snowflake-shaped wool rugs Ms. Frigg had knitted for all the pods in Vingolf. Their snowflake rug had seven points instead of the usual six and was rather misshapen. Still, Sif quite liked it.

"Come hang out," Freya called to her. "We're

playing Crazy Nines, and Idun brought apple tarts from the Valhallateria."

"To cheer us up about not getting any information from the girlgiants at Freya's party after all," added Idun. "Want one?" She motioned with her handful of cards toward a plate of tarts on the rug.

"Thanks," said Sif, still wrapped in her hooded cloak. "Maybe in a minute."

"Better hurry, they're disappearing fast," warned Skade around a bite of tart. She sighed blissfully. "*Mmm.* So did anything come of your trip to the library at least?"

At her mention of the library, Sif felt tears pricking her eyes again. Hunching her shoulders, she turned away from her roomies. "Not really." It was true. She hadn't learned anything about Ragnarok or runes that would necessarily help with the current giant situation.

She wished she could be alone in the pod for a while, but she couldn't very well ask her podmates to leave.

I suppose I should get it over with, she thought miserably. Steeling herself, she turned back to them and said, "You all won't believe what happened to me. It's pretty terrible. Don't laugh." Slowly she lowered her hood. And then burst into sobs.

"What in the nine worlds . . . ?" Skade exclaimed. Freya and Idun stared, momentarily too shocked to speak.

Sif choked back her next sob. "I f-fell asleep in the library. When I woke up, my hair was lying all around me on the floor." No one laughed. Instead her podmates immediately abandoned their card game and tugged Sif down to join them on the rug.

"Sit here," Freya said, bringing her to sit between her and Idun. Sif sat, and immediately Freya and Idun each wrapped an arm around her shoulders, doing their best to comfort her. From her place across the rug, Skade leaned over to join in the group hug. Afterward, she offered up the plate of tarts. Sif shook her head to indicate she didn't want one just now. This caused new tears to flow when she didn't feel her hair sway at her shoulders.

"It'll be okay." Her podmates murmured assurances. "It's just hair." "Aww, poor you."

"Loki got the runeword *klippa* in my Runes class today," Sif managed to say between sobs. Hearing this, the girls drew apart.

"That Loki!" Freya said angrily. "Cutting your hair is exactly the kind of thing he *would* do. After he stole Brising, I wouldn't put anything past him!"

Idun nodded vigorously. "Yeah, like taking one of my magic apples! That guy is nothing but a . . . a . . . *meanie*-pants."

Hearing the supersweet Idun call Loki a name (even a fairly mild one) caused Sif to snicker. Which made the other girls grin.

Skade clenched her fists and jumped up, full of energy. "Let's go confront him! I bet he's back at

Breidablik by now, all happy with himself and thinking he got away with this mean trick."

"Or we could go tell Odin," Idun suggested.

Sif swiped at her eyes to dry them and shook her short-cropped head. It was really weird not to feel her hair swing when she did that. And not weird in a good way. "Not tonight. I'm too tired and upset. And before I accuse Loki, I want to be able to prove he did it." She looked around at her podmates. "I loved my long hair, but it's not just that, you know. I'm worried about what will happen to the wheat crops down in Midgard now that it's gone."

When her podmates gave her puzzled looks, she explained how her goddess powers were bound up in her golden hair, just as she had explained to Thor. "Its growth affects the growth of wheat crops in Midgard. Happy hair, happy wheat, get it?"

"I never knew that," said Freya.

"Me neither," Skade and Idun said together.

Idun offered the plate of apple tarts to Sif again, and this time Sif took one. "Wheat is the main crop in Midgard," she went on. "If the crop fails because of what's happened to my hair, the humans who live there won't have enough to eat. Especially since the giants have been stealing Midgard's wheat."

"Ymir's ears!" Skade exclaimed. "I can see why you're worried!"

"Tell you what," Freya said kindly. "It's dark out now, but we can go down to Midgard after breakfast tomorrow and check on the wheat crops. If they're still healthy, you'll be able to stop worrying."

And if they're not healthy? Sif wanted to ask. But she didn't. What was the point? Without her golden hair, she wouldn't be able to fix things anyway.

As she munched her apple tart in silence, she watched Skade fetch her skis, which were leaning against the podroom wall. Sif could see that she'd painted their bottoms recently with a melted wax mixture that would help them glide faster. After taking a seat on the rug again, Skade began to polish the waxed bottoms with a cloth. "If Loki really is responsible for cutting your hair—and of that I have no doubt—he deserves to be punished!" she declared.

"Agreed!" said Freya. "And not just for what he did to you, Sif, but for all his nasty tricks. He needs to learn a lesson big-time."

Idun nodded. "Right. For everything mean he has ever done to anyone!"

Skade paused in her polishing to punch a fist high in the air. "We're Thunder Girls!" she boomed out. "And that means we make noise when someone does something rotten."

From beside her on the rug, Freya and Idun also punched fists in the air, the three of them fist-bumping to show their power. "Yeah!" said Freya. "We kick up a *storm*!" said Idun.

Sif leaned in and added a fourth fist to the bump.

She couldn't believe how supportive her podmates were being. Their kindness made her tear up again. "Thunder Girls are the best," she told them.

"You bet we are!" said Freya, which made them all crack up.

"So when we find Loki, how do we get him to admit he cut off your hair?" Skade asked. She'd set aside her first ski, and now began to slide her cloth back and forth over the bottom of her second. The best and fastest skier at AA, she skied for a couple of hours a day without fail.

Looking thoughtful, Freya toyed with the strings of one of the pouches she wore. "We should turn the tables on him. Pin him down and cut off all of *his* hair."

"Yeah! But if we try to catch him, he'll transform and escape," Sif said.

"Maybe we could trick him into shape-shifting into something small and slow that we could easily capture," said Idun.

A breeze blew in through the room's open and unshuttered window just then. *Brr!* Sif's head was so cold! She raised her hood again.

At that moment the breeze caused a big ball of dust to roll beneath the lip of Freya's little closet. A goofy grin came over the girlgoddess's face. "I know! How about turning him into a dust bunny!"

Skade looked up from her ski. "Yeah, or how about a skunk? Oh, wait, he's already a skunk." This cracked everyone up again.

Once they'd stopped giggling, Idun, who always liked to think the best of everyone, said, "Maybe we should try to reason with him. If we can get him to put himself in Sif's shoes, surely he'll be sorry for what he did."

"Ha!" Skade exclaimed. "Fat chance. Loki only cares about himself. And when has he *ever* listened to reason?"

"Wait! *Shoes!* That reminds me," Sif said as she finished her last bite of tart. "Loki wore these new speedy magical yellow shoes to class today. If he's wearing them and sees us coming for him, we'll never catch him. He'll just race away."

The cold breeze coming through the window blew back Sif's hood and caused her to shiver again. Noticing, Freya said to her, "Want me to ask Ms. Frigg to knit you a hat till your hair grows back?"

"Sure, how about one with a hundred dangling yellow yarn braids?" Sif suggested with a straight face. "Think it'll fool anyone?"

When the other three girls stared at her, she broke into a laugh. "Kidding! I've already got a knitted hat I can wear, but thanks."

A few minutes later Idun yawned, causing everyone else to yawn too. "Time for bed," Sif said decisively. "I want to go to Midgard as early as possible tomorrow morning to check out the wheat situation."

As the girls tidied up and then got ready for bed, Sif felt much better than when she'd first entered the pod. Even though they hadn't yet figured out what to do about Loki, it was nice to know she had the other girls' support. Her growing feeling of closeness to her pod-mates was the one good thing to come from this!

Soon they were all snuggled down in their hammocklike beds. But despite Sif's tiredness, sleep wouldn't come. For one thing, it was hard getting used to the feel of her short, stubbly hair on her pillow. For another, she was super worried about what the loss of her magic would mean.

Her podbed swayed from side to side as she tossed and turned. In an attempt to calm herself, she absently reached to twist a lock of her hair, but her fingers caught only air, of course. She shivered. Though they'd closed the window, her head was still cold.

Finally she got up, tiptoed over to her closet, and pulled out a knitted hat. After putting it on, she got back in bed. She yawned. Then, remembering what the library runebook had suggested could help her to foresee things in her dreams, she began to whisper the runewords at the heart of her troubles. The Norse words that meant "hair," "wheat," and "giants." *"Hár, hveit, jötnar. Hár, hveit, jötnar,"* she repeated under her breath. She chanted and chanted these words until she fell asleep.

Shortly after she began dozing, a vivid dream came to her. A dream about runes. Written on tiles, like the ones used in Ms. Frigg's Runes class, they fell from the sky like rain. Most landed upside down on the ground, their blank sides up, but the ones that landed right-side up formed words.

Sif groaned in her sleep when *klippa* was spelled out over and over again. But then a wind came up and her dream changed. Most of the tiles turned into dry leaves and were swept away by the wind. Now only ten tiles remained, all blank-side up. One by one they flipped over as if turned by an unseen hand. In her dream Sif stared at the line of ten runes, trying to make sense of them. Suddenly a pair of scissors appeared. They didn't cut anything, though. Instead they nudged the rune tiles around, separating them into a set of six and a set of four.

Sif continued to dream, her eyes fluttering as she read the resulting two runewords: *dvergr* and *gjöf*. "Dwarf" and "gift." The two words repeated themselves in her head over and over, and each time she saw the scissors flashing down between them. Even slumbering, she knew she was having a prophetic dream! One that was trying to tell her something important. But what?

Then abruptly the dream's meaning crystallized. It was telling her what she must get Loki to do! Now the scissors disappeared. The wind brushed away the ten tiles. As the dream came to an end, Sif sighed softly. Though she was still asleep, a small smile curved her lips.

7
Caught!

SIF WOKE LATER THAN SHE'D MEANT TO THE
next morning. Luckily, it was Saturday, so there weren't
any classes she had to hurry to get ready for when she
finally tumbled out of bed. She glanced around and saw
that the other three Thunder Girls were already gone
from their pod.

First thing, she whipped off her knitted hat. Then
she forced herself to look squarely at her image in the
mirror that hung from her closet door. She frowned at

112

the way her hair stuck up like golden bristles all over her head. Some others might find the short style cute, she supposed. She might too, on somebody else! She'd always had long hair, though, and was unused to this new look. She tried to pat the bristles down, but it was hopeless. They just sprang up again. Whatever! If she had to have short hair, she was going to rock it!

She slipped several colorful ribbons around her head and then tied them together at the top in a cute bow. Then she dressed quickly, slipping into a fresh linen shift and her navy *hangerock*. While busily fastening the straps with silver brooches, she began to wonder if her pod-mates had already gone to breakfast at the V. But then the pod door opened and Freya stuck her blond head in around the frame.

"Oh good. You're up. Love the ribbons!" she said brightly. "I've just been sitting with my cats in the common area. Coming out? It's nice and warm. There's a big fire burning in the pit." Without waiting for a reply, she added, "We didn't want to wake you since you were sleeping so hard. So Idun headed to Midgard Mall early and plans to check on the wheat fields for you. I'm waiting for Skade to get back from her morning ski run. Then maybe the three of us can go to breakfast? Idun should be back soon with news."

"Okay. I'll be right out," Sif said. There would be girls from other pods in the communal room who didn't yet know what had happened to her last night. And she was still feeling sensitive about her appearance, despite the ribbons. So she grabbed her wool hat from the top shelf of her closet and jammed it down over her head, ribbons and all, before leaving the pod.

As Sif ventured into the communal room, a light-elf from the Northern Lights pod and a girlgiant from the Polar Bears looked up from a table where they sat playing a board game. It was called *Halatafl* and involved jumping pegs around in the holes on the board. The two red pegs stood for foxes, and the many yellow pegs were sheep. The fox player could win by capturing all the sheep. But if the sheep player managed to fill the paddock on the board first, the sheep player won.

The sparkly lights in the light-elf's hair twinkled as she and the girlgiant nodded to Sif, but then they went back to playing their game. Since they hadn't looked curious and had barely glanced at her, Sif guessed her podmates hadn't told them about her shorn hair. The two girls probably thought her long golden hair was tucked up under her cap. If only!

With her two gray tabby cats curled up in her lap now, Freya was sitting on a low stool before the blazing fire at the center of the big, round room. Sif picked up the nearest free stool, plunked it down next to Freya's, and sat.

Freya's eyes flicked to Sif's navy knitted hat. In a sympathetic voice she asked, "How are you doing?"

Sif shrugged and sent her a weak smile. "I'll survive, thanks."

Just then they heard the front door of Vingolf bang

open. Seconds later Skade tromped through the inner door carrying her skis and wearing snow-encrusted boots. She was accompanied by a stiff cold wind that swirled through the communal room.

"*Brr.* Did you leave the outside door open again?" Sif called out to Skade, who halted in her tracks. Still holding her skis, she was using her teeth to pull off her mittens.

"Oh, yeah. Sorry," Skade mumbled through a mouthful of mitten.

"What's the matter with you?" Freya teased the girl. "Were you born in a barn?"

"Nope," Skade replied good-naturedly as she stuffed her mittens inside the pocket of her cloak. "But the giant side of my family in Jotunheim *has* a barn."

The three podmates laughed. Some giants and half-giants, could be quite grumpy, such as Angerboda from Sif's Runes class. Good thing Skade wasn't like that. Oh, she could be forceful when the occasion called for it, but she was also reasonable.

Skade clomped back out to close the front door, and this time she left her skis in the mudroom. Once back, she rubbed her hands together to warm them as she stomped toward the fire.

"Boots off," Freya reminded her. "They're leaving water on the floor."

"Oh, yeah." Skade stripped off the sparkly red boots and let them drop to the floor.

"Boot racks," Sif reminded her.

"Oh, yeah." Skade swept up the boots and went to leave them on the mudroom racks. Meanwhile, Sif and Freya exchanged amused looks.

When Skade returned to join them, she pulled her mittens from the pocket of her cloak and then placed them near the fire to dry. Speaking in a low voice so that the girls playing *Halatafl* wouldn't overhear, she announced, "So guess who I saw walking toward the Valhallateria on my way back from skiing? Loki!"

"That rat!" huffed Freya. Surprised by the vehemence

in her voice, or maybe recognizing the word "rat," her cats looked up at her in surprise. "It's okay, *silfrkatter*," she reassured them, using a word that meant "silver cats." "Nothing for you to be concerned about." She stroked her hands along both their backs, and they settled again to purr in low rumbles.

"He *is* a rat. Loki the ratski." Skade pulled a stool close to them and the fire and sat. "He was just walking along, whistling and smiling, acting like he hadn't done anything wrong."

After a pause Sif leaned toward her two podmates. "Last night I had a prophetic dream. It was about Loki, I think," she whispered to them. Immediately they bent forward to listen. "There's something I have to get him to do," Sif went on. "To make up for the tricks he's pulled on all of us. But I'll need your help. Can you guys do something for me right now? Before breakfast?"

"Sure," Skade said in a low voice.

Freya nodded enthusiastically. "Name it!"

"So I need you to go to Breidablik . . . ," Sif began telling the girls. They listened eagerly as she outlined the first part of a larger plan she'd come up with, the details of which she promised to reveal later.

Not long after, the three girls left Vingolf Hall. Freya and Skade went in one direction, while Sif went in another, making her way to the Valhallateria. Thor was heading inside as she arrived, so he held the door open for her and then followed her in.

"That Loki!" He pointed to where the boygod sat laughing with a bunch of other boys at a table across the room. "Look at him pretending like he didn't do anything." Thor's jaw tightened. "I'd like to go over there and knock him into next week."

Sif giggled. It was nice of Thor to stand up for her, but he sure did have a stormy temper! "Hold on to your Belt-o'-Power there, boygod," she said with a grin. "I have another idea instead. And I could use your help." As she told him what she wanted him to do, she hoped her request would give him something else to focus on besides starting a fight.

Thor nodded, looking pleased to help and glad to have some action he could take. "You can count on me."

Just as Sif finished telling him about the errand she'd sent Freya and Skade on, the two girls showed up. "Got 'em," Freya announced, patting her bulging pocket.

Skade grinned. "Yeah, easy peasy. We asked Bragi, and he . . ." Breaking off suddenly, she glanced over at Thor, a question in her eyes.

"It's okay," Sif hastened to assure both girls. "I told Thor about you going to Breidablik. He's going to help us."

"Cool," said Skade, shooting the boygod an approving glance. "So anyway, Bragi got what we wanted right off of Loki's desk."

"With the evidence still stuck to them," Freya added in a satisfied voice. "We are *so* going to nail him!"

Sif, Thor, and the other two girls all swung their

heads at the same time to look at Loki. Luckily, he was too busy laughing and chatting to notice.

Thor grunted in annoyance. "Now?" he asked Sif.

"Now," she replied, nodding.

With determined looks on their faces, the four quickly closed in on Loki. He had just grabbed a Valkyrie's tray to tease her—the perfect distraction they needed to corner that slippery boygod of fire. They wouldn't let him wiggle out of this!

A hush settled over Loki's table as Thor placed a heavy hand on the boy's shoulder. Loki startled, and the Valkyrie used that opportunity to wrench her tray from his grasp. She stuck out her tongue at him before moving off to deliver food to another table.

"Hey," Loki protested as he glanced up at Thor. He tried to rise from the table, but Thor's grip kept him in his seat.

"Ha! Even those speedy yellow shoes of yours aren't going to help you now!" Thor thundered. "You're not going anywhere. Not shape-shifting, either." The touch of Thor's hand was grounding the wily boygod as per the rules of magic, making transforming to another shape impossible.

Thor's booming voice got the attention of every student in the V, as well as the painted warrior figures in the wooden friezes that covered the walls. All eyes turned expectantly toward Loki, Thor, and the three girlgoddesses standing near them.

"I fell asleep in the library after dinner last night!" Sif announced to the entire room in a clear, loud voice. "And when I woke up, I discovered that *someone*"—and here she gave Loki a long, hard look—"had cut . . . off . . . my . . . hair!"

Dramatically Sif whipped off her knitted hat. The ribbons she'd tied around her head stayed in place. Gasps swept the room as students and warriors alike stared with shock and curiosity at Sif's short-cropped hair. She hadn't really wanted to make such a public display of herself, but it was necessary. Her head was part of the evidence she hoped would do Loki in!

"I know how to rock this short cut, right?" she said, grinning with all the confidence she could muster and giving her new do a quick fluff with one hand. But then she scowled. "Thing is, this was not my choice."

Loki gulped and tried to rise again. When Thor kept his hand firmly on the boygod's shoulder, Loki decided to try his charm on Sif. "Come on," he whined. "This is unfair. I didn't cut your hair!"

Freya glared at him and chimed in with, "Oh really?" With a dramatic flourish, she whipped the evidence from her *hangerock* pocket: a pair of scissors. Holding them up for all to see, she made a cutting motion in the air for effect. *Snip! Snip!*

Sif stared at the scissors in surprise. Because they looked exactly like the ones she'd seen in her dream last night!

"And guess where we found these scissors?" Skade

continued to the room in general. Then she pointed at Loki. "In *his* pod."

"On top of his desk," added Freya.

The students and warriors in the V began to mutter among themselves.

Loki's face went a little pale. But then, recovering some of his old swagger, he scoffed. "So? What does that prove? Everyone owns scissors. They're part of our AA school supplies!"

"True," Freya said. "But look what we found stuck to the blades of *yours*!" She plucked a few long golden hairs caught in the scissors and held them up. They glistened in the sunlight coming through the windows of the Valhallateria.

"Aha! That's my hair!" declared Sif.

Though not everyone could see the strands, those closest to Freya did, and they gasped. The muttering among the students grew louder and more condemning.

"So what? Still doesn't prove anything," Loki whined,

but he avoided looking at Sif. He knew what he'd done and that it was wrong. But being who he was, he just couldn't stop trying to weasel his way out of trouble.

A little self-conscious when everyone's eyes shifted her way again, Sif slipped her knitted hat back on. She'd made her point, but mostly, her head was chilly now that her long hair was gone.

Speaking to the room at large once more, she announced, "Many of you may not know this, but my hair is the source of my girlgoddess powers. Its health ensures there's a good wheat harvest in Midgard each year." While speaking, she faced different directions so that all would be able to see and hear her well. Abruptly she whipped around toward Loki again. "Now that my hair is gone, I worry about what's going to happen to the wheat!"

Another, louder murmur of concern ran through the Valhallateria.

"I'll tell you what has *already* happened to it!" a new

voice called out. Idun was back! As she and a couple of other girlgoddesses entered the dining hall, all heads swung their way. Anger had apparently overcome her usual shyness for the moment. Boldly she continued, her eyes flashing. "We just came from Midgard, where we saw fields and fields of withering wheat. It's a disaster!"

A low, angry sound escaped Thor's throat. "Frost giants from Jotunheim have been stealing Midgard's wheat and storing it up for the last couple of weeks." With his hand still pressed down firmly on Loki's shoulder, he narrowed his eyes accusingly at the boygod. "It's almost like those giants knew this would happen and were planning ahead."

"Argh! So they were plotting this all along," Sif heard Skade mutter.

Now one of the Valkyries spoke up. "Even Asgard depends on Midgard's wheat! Without it, we won't be able to make bread in our kitchen here at the academy, either. No one in any of the worlds—except maybe

Jotunheim—will be able to bake anything that requires wheat flour."

As what she'd said sank in, angry grumbles arose among the AA students. After all, bread was a huge part of every meal, and without flour there would also be no more gravies, puddings—or desserts!

Around the V, shouts rang out. "It's Loki's fault!" "He's probably in cahoots with the giants!" "He's guilty!" "He cut Sif's hair on purpose so the wheat would die!" "The giants will feast on the wheat they stole, and make everyone else pay high prices to buy some of it from them!"

The hundreds of warriors that inhabited the sculpted wooden friezes had become more and more agitated as talk continued. All at once one of the warriors picked up a rotten apple from a table within his frieze. His hand reached out from the frieze and threw it straight at Loki.

"Hey!" Loki managed to duck in his seat, dodging the apple. When he tried to rise from the table once more, Thor gave his shoulder an even tighter squeeze to make sure he stayed put.

As other warriors drew their arms back to lob more of the food decorating their friezes at Loki, Thor shouted, "Hold your fire! For now." Luckily, they obeyed.

"Well, Loki?" Sif called out in as loud and stern a voice as she could muster. "How are you going to fix this?" To illustrate her meaning, she pointed to a loaf of bread on the table. "And this?" Now she pointed at her hat-covered head. "Or should we all go talk to Odin about it?" she added fiercely.

Loki's eyes bugged out. Knowing that Odin would likely deal harshly with him, he tried to come up with an idea to save himself. "Okay, I'm not admitting to anything, but . . ." He broke off, as if something had just come to him. Brightening a bit, he snapped his fingers. "Tell you what. I'll go to the dwarfs in Darkalfheim. They have tons of gold hidden in their caves. I'll get them to forge new hair out of gold for you, Sif. And I'll have them infuse it with magic so the crops in Midgard will grow again!"

"And exactly how do you plan to convince them to do that?" demanded Skade.

Loki wiggled his eyebrows mischievously. "With my winning personality, of course!"

Sif and her three podmates all rolled their eyes.

"Why should we believe you?" someone else exclaimed. "You'd say anything to avoid getting in trouble with Odin!"

"Yeah," chorused most of the students and warriors. More angry rumbling swept the room.

Sif held up her hand for quiet. One of the two rune-words from her dream had been *dvergr*, for "dwarf." She felt certain the dream must've been prophesying what Loki was now proposing, and that convinced her to give the crafty boygod a chance to make things right.

"Okay," she told him. "Visit the dwarfs."

Her podmates, Thor, and nearly everyone else in

the Valhallateria all stared at her in surprise.

"Do you really trust him?" Skade blurted out.

"Even if he does what he says, it's not enough to make up for the trouble he's caused," Freya protested.

Loki blinked. Looking at Sif, he said plaintively, "What more can I do?"

Sif's eyes swept over all those assembled in the V before settling again on Loki. She had leverage right now and needed to use it. The other runeword from her dream had been *gjöf* (for "gift").

"Besides new hair for me, you have to promise to get the dwarfs to make us some gifts while they're at it," she told him. "Gifts that we at the academy can use to help fight the giants you've riled up and keep Asgard safe!"

When students and warriors cheered her idea, she smiled.

Loki groaned. "And how am I supposed to do that?" At this question an overripe plum sailed toward his head from out of one of the friezes. Before Loki could duck, the plum smacked him squarely on the forehead. Red juice dripped down his nose. "Okay, okay. Give me a minute. I'm thinking," Loki whined as he wiped at his face.

Sif pressed on, knowing she had the upper hand. "You heard my deal, Loki. I'm sure you'll figure out a way to get those gifts."

Loki smiled a little and even puffed out his chest. He prided himself on his cleverness, she knew. "You're right, I will!" he exclaimed. Speaking earnestly to Sif, he said, "Your hair will be good as new. No, *better* than new . . . in no time at all."

"I'll hold you to that," she told him. "And don't forget the gifts." She held up a hand with fingers spread wide. "Five of them should do it. Besides my new hair, that is."

"Six things in all?" Loki grumped. A hand in one of the friezes drew back, holding a peach. Noticing it, Loki yelled, "Wait! I agree, I agree!"

Sif gestured to Thor to let Loki go. Reluctantly Thor did. Immediately Loki leaped from his seat. In seconds he'd raced out of the V in his magical yellow shoes, which could skim over land and water.

The question was, Sif thought as she watched him go, would he do what he'd promised?

8
Land of the Dwarfs

AFTER LOKI HAD RUN OFF, EVERYONE IN
the V began to discuss the bargain he'd made. Sif
could hear students muttering about the dire actions
they would take if that boygod didn't come through
with gifts for the gods and new hair for Sif.

Recalling Skade's earlier question, Sif leaned over to
Freya. "Think we can trust Loki to come through?"

Freya sighed. "Not really."

Caw! Caw! Just then Hugin and Munin, two

magical ravens who flew out over the worlds every day to collect news for Odin, soared into the Valhallateria through an open window. *Whoosh!* They glided down toward the middle of the room, their large black wings flapping as they landed atop the big ceramic goat fountain.

The students went quiet as they watched the ravens hop lower on the fountain and open their beaks under two of the spigots to help themselves to a drink. When they'd finished, the two ravens flapped up to sit on top of Heidrun again. Cocking their heads, they beadily eyed the students, who cautiously went back to talking among themselves about topics other than Loki. Because whatever Hugin and Munin saw and heard, they would whisper in Odin's ears when they returned to perch on his shoulders. And the students wouldn't go to Odin with all of this . . . yet. Not unless Loki bailed on his promises.

"Should we follow Loki to Darkalfheim?" Freya

whispered to Sif while the ravens were busy watching other students.

"Couldn't hurt," Sif replied. Since they hadn't had breakfast yet, the two girls grabbed a couple of apple fritters off a tray on the nearest table before they edged toward the door. They sent Idun and Skade quick waves. Then, on silent feet, they slipped out of the dining hall.

Sif glanced over at Freya as they hurried off along a branchway. "You're probably wondering why I agreed so easily to Loki's idea to go see the dwarfs," she said, her words causing fog-puffs in the cold air. "It's because I saw the runewords for 'dwarf,' and 'gift,' in my prophetic dream last night."

"Really?" said Freya, sounding intrigued. "So you foresaw his trip to the dwarfs to get gifts."

Sif nodded. "I think so. The prophecy was kind of vague, though."

"Prophecies usually are," Freya replied.

Sif took a big bite of her apple fritter as they hurried along. "Mmm. I'm *really* going to miss these if we can't save the wheat."

Freya was chowing down on her fritter as well. "Me too," she said between bites. "Hey! Want to use my cart to get to Darkalfheim?"

"Sure, it'll be way faster than walking. I know you don't like to fly very high in your cart, though, so first let me take my swan shape. I'll flap up and see if I can spot Loki from the air."

Sif concentrated, trying to shape-shift. To her surprise, nothing happened. She tried again. And again. But the more she tried to summon the magic that would transform her, the more exhausted and weak she became.

Finally, after her fifth try, she stopped. "I . . . I can't do it," she admitted to Freya at last. "Cutting my hair must've completely drained my magic. This is awful!"

"Hey, don't worry," Freya said soothingly. She patted Sif's arm. "We'll get your powers back, one way or another!" So saying, she pulled up a pouch that dangled from one of her necklaces. Before she'd left the girls' dorm that morning, she'd shrunk her two magical cats into the beautiful cat's-eye marble she kept in that pouch.

Now Freya shook out the marble and tossed it in the air, chanting, "Here, kitty, kitty."

Plink! Instantly the two gray tabby cats appeared, along with a magical red cart. Both cats and cart grew and grew, until the cats were the size of lions and the cart was large enough to seat as many as four people.

"Remember, I'm still kind of new at this, so cut my carting skills some slack," Freya warned as they hopped in. (She'd gotten her magical cat's-eye marble just a couple of days before coming to AA.) Without waiting for Sif to respond, Freya commanded, "Fly, kitty, kitty!"

The cart gave a lurch and they were off! *Meow! Meow!* Whoa! It was like herding cats to get the two tabbies to pull the cart in the direction the girls wanted to go. Flying a half dozen feet above the branchway, those cats zigzagged from side to side, almost causing the cart to collide with tree trunks a couple of times. But at last they soared over the Bifrost Bridge and followed it all the way down to the worlds on the second ring.

When Midgard's fields came into view, it was as Idun had said. The wheat had withered. The stalks were thin and scraggly, and the heads were bent and sickly looking. Horrified, Sif sucked in her breath. Freya reached over to squeeze her hand reassuringly. "Don't worry. Your powers will return as soon as Loki gets the dwarfs to make you some new hair."

"Hope so," said Sif. Still, she couldn't help being worried. There had been nothing in her dream to indicate that Loki's trip to the dwarfs would result in a return of her goddess powers. And what would dwarf-made hair be like, anyway? Would it be weird and limp, or stiff as a broom? Anything would be better than this slow-growing porcupine hair, though! She poked a finger under her knitted hat and rubbed at the unfamiliar, itchy short spikes.

"To Darkalfheim, *silfrkatter*!" Freya commanded. In response the cats extended their claws and made an abrupt turn to head for a craggy black peak in the distance. As they drew closer, the girls noticed a sign atop the peak that read DARKALFHEIM: KEEP OUT!

Ignoring the warning, Freya called out to her cats, "Onward!" While flying above a well-worn path, they passed a glacier and ducked under an overhanging cliff. Then they headed steeply down, down, down, before eventually finding themselves near the opening to a labyrinth of caves that burrowed beneath the earth, part of the land of the dwarfs.

Ahead the two girls caught sight of Loki gliding toward the caves in his magical shoes. "Keep back! We don't want him to see us!" Sif warned.

"Whoa, kitty, kitty!" Freya called softly. Their landing was bumpy, a series of hard bounces, but she succeeded in getting her cats to set down among some trees about a hundred feet away from the caves.

Quickly both girls jumped from the cart. "Good job, *silfrkatter*," Freya praised, giving her pets head rubs that made them grin. Then she commanded, "Catnap!"

Plink! In the blink of an eye, both cart and cats shrank into a cat's-eye marble again. She snatched the magical marble out of midair before it could fall to the ground, then slipped it back in its pouch.

The girls peeked out from between the trees and watched Loki slip inside one of the caves. "I know that cave!" said Freya. "It's where I found Brising after Ivaldi's sons stole it." The dwarf Ivaldi had once been famed for his metalworking skills. His four sons were said to be every bit as talented. And judging from the gorgeous jeweled necklace they'd made and set Freya's magic jewel in, Sif was inclined to believe it!

She and Freya left their hiding place and, following Loki, passed by a row of stone columns. Leading to who knew where, they were ranged along a dirt path that ran parallel to the cave system, between it and the trees they'd landed among. Just before the girls entered the dark cave, they heard a loud *Caw! Caw!* They looked up. Odin's two ravens were perched on the cliff above the cave, staring down at them.

"Uh-oh," said Sif as they hurried inside. "Looks like Hugin and Munin followed us. Think Odin might have found out about my hair? And the bargain we made with Loki? Maybe he sent those ravens to keep tabs on the situation?"

Freya slowed her steps to adjust to the sudden darkness, and shrugged. "Well, Odin's eye *is* all seeing." (The academy principal had a single eye that could see all around the worlds!) "Between that eye and those birds of his, it's hard to keep secrets from him for long."

Their discussion was interrupted by a clanging sound that came from somewhere deep inside the cave they were in. Ahead in the distance orange and yellow sparks flew, lighting up the inky blackness. A forge! The girls held hands and felt their way along the cave's cold, uneven wall in the direction of the sparks.

As they got closer, they heard voices. One was Loki's.

"I know what I'm asking would be a hard task for any other dwarf," he wheedled. Obviously, he was talking to one of the dwarf brothers who ran the forge. "But spinning gold to make new hair for the girlgoddess Sif will be as *easy as pie* for you, Alfrigg. Your craftsmanship is unbeatable," Loki declared, laying the compliments on thick.

The open arched doorway to the forge was now no more than twenty feet ahead of the girls. After going closer still, they stopped to listen by a huge mountain of coal that was stacked just outside the entrance. Sif scanned the sign above the arch:

Ivaldi's Sons:

Superfine Blacksmithing

(Way Better Than the Other Guys!)

"What other guys?" Sif whispered to Freya.

Instead of answering, Freya held a finger to her lips. The two girls craned their necks to peek inside the forge without being seen. Sif noticed portraits of four dwarfs above the forge. Their names were written in gold leaf below the portraits. A good way to let visitors know who was who! Like most dwarfs, these wore colorful caps, leather-and-gold bracelets, and pointed boots. And they were all a foot or so shorter than the girls.

"Humph. All that is true. But why should my brothers and I do you any favors?" the dwarf named Alfrigg replied. He seemed to be in charge here, Sif decided.

The dwarf named Berling (according to the portrait) yelled to the one named Dvalin, "DID LOKI SAY HE WANTS AN EASY PIE? WE'RE NOT BAKERS!"

"No! He said he wants us to spin some hair!" Dvalin shouted back at him.

A fourth dwarf brother, Grerr, cocked his head curiously. "How did Sif lose her hair, anyway?"

"SIF LOST A CHAIR?" Berling asked.

The other dwarfs ignored him. "It was, uh, some kind of hairstyling accident," Loki hedged. "You know how girls are, always trying to get more beautiful."

"Ugh! As if!" Sif whispered furiously to Freya.

"Yeah, figures he wouldn't fess up that he whacked off your hair," Freya said in a low but equally angry voice. "Or maybe he's afraid that if they knew he was responsible, they wouldn't help him."

Deciding that was possible, Sif cooled down a little and moved a bit closer to see what was going on. Unfortunately, while doing this, she accidentally elbowed the stack of coal. Chunks of it began raining down on them. *Boom! Boom!* "HEY, WHAT WAS THAT?" Deaf as he was, even Berling could hear the coal fall.

To avoid getting crushed, the girls made a run for it, zipping across the arched opening to stand with their backs pressed against the cave wall at the opposite side of the entrance. Heart pounding, Sif held up crossed fingers to Freya, who nodded in return. They were both hoping none of the dwarfs had seen their mad dash or would come out to check on the coal.

If the girlgoddesses got caught listening in, it might ruin the entire deal Loki was trying to make! As the most scheming and persuasive of the gods by far, he would have the best chance of anyone at getting the dwarfs to make both new hair for Sif and those other gifts.

Luckily, Alfrigg was unfazed by a few pieces of falling coal. He distracted Berling before he could go investigate, shouting, "Put that thing back in the forge, Berly Whirly! It's obviously not ready yet. Looks like something that got pecked by a woodpecker, then mauled by dragon claws!"

"Phew," Freya whispered. They were in the clear.

Taking a new tack now, Loki said to Alfrigg, "Just think how pleased the gods and goddesses of Asgard will be if you do what I'm asking. Especially Odin. He rewards those he considers his friends."

Peeking in, the girls saw Alfrigg cross his muscular arms. "Humph. What have the gods ever done for me?"

"And I'll owe you a favor, too," Loki hastened to add. "No expiration date."

The grumpy dwarf snorted. "Promises, promises!"

"Hey! What's the big deal, Alfrigg? The forge is already hot," said Dvalin. "Let's make the girl some hair, for dwarf's sake!"

"Yeah, Odin would be a good ally to have, and a favor from Loki could be . . . *useful*," said Grerr.

"Maybe you're right," Alfrigg said, stroking his beard thoughtfully. "Okay! We'll do it."

"Awesome!" Loki declared. Though the girls couldn't see him from where they stood, Sif pictured him rubbing his hands together with glee now that he'd gotten his way. "And if you could add in some gifts—say, a spear that never misses its goal, for Odin, and a ship that can sail over land and sea, and—"

Alfrigg let out an annoyed grunt. "You're pushing your luck, Tricky-Loki!"

It was a nickname that was well deserved, Sif thought. However, she did like Loki's gift ideas so far!

"Oh, but just think how pleased the gods and goddesses will be with those gifts!" Loki exclaimed. "They'll sing your praises far and wide. It'll be like free advertising! In no time you'll become known as the best smiths in all the nine worlds. Everyone will flock to your cave with all sorts of projects for you. They'll ignore your competitors' workshops!"

Hidden in the shadows, Sif and Freya shared a grin. When it suited him, no one was more convincing than Loki.

At the notion of outdoing other blacksmiths, Alfrigg grew more enthusiastic. "Yeah! But none of you Aesir better come asking for more freebies after this."

"We . . . um . . . *I* . . . won't mention the gifts were

free when I speak of them," Loki assured him quickly.

"Okay. Deal," agreed Alfrigg at last.

"We're running low on coal," said Dvalin. "I'll go get some before we start."

Hearing this, the girls crept from their hiding place and rushed back up the passageway to the cave's entrance before the dwarf could catch them listening in. Once outside, they high-fived. The plan seemed to be working!

Freya reached for the pouch that contained her cat's-eye marble. "Since Loki's actually doing what he's supposed to, shall we go ahead and leave?"

Sif glanced up at the cliff, noting that Odin's two ravens had flown off. Then she replied to Freya, "Did you notice the dwarfs only agreed to make *two* gifts in addition to spinning me some new hair? Let's wait here and make sure Loki talked them into making five, plus my hair, as he promised us."

Freya gave a nod. "Good point. In fact, maybe we should nab the gifts from him the minute he comes out of the cave and deliver them to the academy ourselves. Because I wouldn't put it past Loki to claim they were never made and just keep them for himself!"

"Neither would I," Sif agreed. "Let's do it!" The girls parked themselves on a large rock behind one of the stone columns they'd passed earlier. Thus hidden, they waited for Loki to come out.

Turned out that the Ivaldi brothers were not only skilled; they were *fast*. Loki ambled out of the cave only a half hour later carrying a large bag. A sharp-looking spear was pointing out its top. Even from a distance the girls could hear him whistling merrily and see that he looked quite pleased with himself.

"That bag is way too small to fit that spear, plus a ship, some hair, and three more gifts," Sif whispered to Freya while Loki was still some ways off.

"The bag could be magical," Freya replied. "Maybe it can shrink stuff to fit. You know, like how my cart and cats can shrink to a marble to fit in a pouch."

"We need to find out," whispered Sif.

Freya nodded. "Let's sneak up on Loki and grab his arms so he won't be able to transform or race off. Then we'll check the number of gifts and transport the bag back to the academy in my cart if he got all six, including your new hair."

"Okay, but we can't let him spot us or there'll be no way we can catch him," Sif advised.

As Loki drew closer, the girls got ready to spring out at him. But to their surprise, he swerved before he reached the column nearest them. Walking at a diagonal, he bypassed several other stone columns before joining the path they ranged along.

"Hey!" Sif whispered to Freya. "Where's he going?"

Freya shrugged. "I don't know. But he's not heading back to the academy, that's for sure!"

9
The Bet

QUIETLY SIF AND FREYA BEGAN TO FOLLOW
Loki along the dirt path. Darting from stone column to
stone column, they paused to hide behind each, hoping
to keep him from spotting them too soon. Luckily, the
boygod never looked back.

At the end of the path, quite out in the open but
with a mountain behind it, was a large wooden building.
A metal sign hung above the doorway. It read:

Brokk and Sindri:

Finest Blacksmith Brothers Ever

(Way Better Than Those Other Guys!)

Beneath this was a motto: WE STRIKE WHEN THE IRON IS HOT. And indeed, the girls could hear hammers clanging away inside. They watched Loki enter the building, and then moved closer.

There weren't any windows along the front, but spying a small open window on the side of the building, they sneaked over and peeked through. Sparks of fire were flying as a squat, muscular dwarf with a dark beard and wavy black hair hammered away at a glowing lump of metal he held between tongs on top of a heavy iron anvil. There were *two* portraits over the forge here. A glance at the nameplates beneath each showed that this dwarf was named Sindri.

Nearby stood the other blacksmith brother, Brokk. He was bald on top, with a fringe of orange hair ringing his head. He stopped whatever he'd been doing to come over to Loki. "Whatcha got there?" he asked as the boy-god set down his bag.

"Just you wait and see," Loki said mischievously. Sif's and Freya's eyes widened when he removed the sharp spear that had been sticking out from the top of the bag and then took out a beautiful golden skein of hair.

At the sight of it, Sif huffed loudly. Was Loki planning to trade the hair and other gifts to these dwarfs for his own gain?

Freya quickly clapped a hand over Sif's mouth. When she let go, Sif hissed, "What's Loki doing? That hair is *mine*. Those other dwarfs made it for *me*!"

"Shh," cautioned Freya. "We'll make sure you get your hair. For now, let's find out what Loki is up to. He's only pulled two gifts from that bag so far."

Freya was right. Loki was still four gifts shy of the number he'd promised to bring back. And the bag looked almost empty! Sif calmed herself as they waited to see what the boygod would do next.

By now Sindri had set down his hammer and tongs in order to examine the treasures Loki had taken out of the bag. When Loki put the golden skein of hair—*her* hair—in the dwarf's grimy, coal-blackened hands, Sif had to stifle an urge to pound on the window and protest. But she forced herself not to interrupt. As Freya had said, they needed to find out what Loki was up to. Right now they had no proof of what that was.

"Wow!" said Brokk, gazing in wonder at what Sindri held. "Hair? Made from *real* gold!"

"You betcha! Ah, but that's not all! I've saved the best for last," Loki exclaimed. As the blacksmith brothers gathered around, he drew a leather pouch from his bag and opened it. It was much like the ones hanging from Freya's necklaces, only several times larger. Quickly he pulled an object from the pouch that seemed to be a jumble of many small parts.

"What do you think that is?" Sif whispered to Freya as they continued to stare through the window.

"No clue," Freya replied uncertainly.

The two brothers appeared to be just as confused. Sindri stared at the object with raised eyebrows as Loki proceeded to unfold its many small parts. Finally those parts clicked into place to become the cunning little ship Loki had requested.

"It's magical, of course. Once in water, it will grow to an enormous size," Loki informed them. "So huge that it can carry hundreds of crew, their supplies, and weapons. Plus, I have been assured that a good wind is guaranteed to blow whenever the ship's sail is raised."

Cool, Sif mouthed silently, and Freya nodded.

Sindri scowled. "Assured by who? Ivaldi's sons?" When Loki just smiled in response, Brokk picked up the ship, and the two dwarfs murmured over it, obviously as impressed by it as Sif and Freya were.

"Hair. Ship. Spear. That's only *three* gifts," Sif

whispered. Then a new thought came to her. "I think Loki must be planning to—"

Shh. Freya held a finger to her lips as Loki began to speak again. "I bet you've never seen such well-crafted treasures as these, have you?" he asked.

"Humph. The work done in our shop is finer," Sindri declared flatly. But to Sif's ear, he sounded unsure. Maybe even a little jealous.

"Think so?" Loki said skeptically. "Admit it. You guys could never make objects as awesome as these. They're gifts for the gods of Asgard!" He slapped Brokk on the back, which, much to Sif's horror, caused him to fumble the ship and nearly drop it.

"Ha! Can too make better gifts! Want to bet?" Sindri challenged. As Loki repacked his bag with Sif's hair, the ship, and the spear, Brokk began banging at his anvil while still keeping an eye on the drama that was unfolding.

Sif and Freya grinned at each other. Because both

had just figured out what Loki was up to. He wasn't going to trade these three gifts for his own gain. Not at all. Instead he was going to try to trick these brothers into creating *more* gifts for the gods. *Three* more, to be exact. Gifts that could help protect the academy against enemy giants and delay the coming of Ragnarok and the downfall of Yggdrasil!

Loki screwed up his face, as if considering Sindri's idea. "Okay," he said at last. "I'm so sure you guys *cannot* create anything to rival these three gifts that I'll stake my head on it."

Sif and Freya gasped at Loki's daring wager and then ducked below the edge of the window as the very thing that Loki had just staked in his bet turned their way. Had he heard them? Hopefully not, since Brokk had been hammering.

When Loki said nothing more and no one came out of the shop, the girls popped up their heads to peek again. Looking stunned, Brokk had stopped hammering, and both brothers were staring at Loki. Sindri's bushy black eyebrows rose in disbelief. "If our gifts are more magnificent than the Ivaldi brothers' gifts, you'll give us your *head*? What are we going to do with that?"

"Put it on a shelf for decoration?" Loki joked.

Brokk appeared to consider the offer. "A god's head *would* be quite a trophy."

Sindri nodded. "I guess our workshop *could* do with some freshening up." He said this quite seriously.

Sif and Freya listened in shock as the two dwarfs began discussing exactly how they would mount Loki's head and where it would look best. Having settled on the idea, they both grabbed their tongs and chorused, "It's a deal!"

Sindri's tongs still held the lump of metal he'd been hammering earlier, so now he stuck it in the red-hot forge till it softened and began to glow again. Then he returned the lump to his anvil and picked up his hammer. *Clang, clang, clang.*

"One question," Brokk said to Loki, his tongs in hand too. "Who will do the judging to decide which blacksmith shop's gifts are the best?"

"How about Odin?" Loki suggested.

CLANK! Sindri brought his hammer down so hard, it smashed the object he'd been making to smithereens and caused Sif and Freya to jump in surprise. "No way!" he bellowed.

"Yeah! Why should we trust him? He'll take your side," said Brokk.

Loki shrugged. "Odin has no problem with you dwarfs. It's the giants who are his enemies, so why would he favor me, a *half-giant*, over you?"

"Makes sense," Sindri said after a few moments spent stroking his beard.

"Agreed," said Brokk. "Odin can judge."

Loki grinned. It seemed his legendary powers of persuasion had triumphed again, Sif thought. Despite what he'd told the dwarfs, he was probably certain of his ability to convince Odin to favor him, and so he'd keep his head.

As Sindri got to work heating a new lump of metal in the forge, Loki hovered nearby, making remarks such as "Ymir's bones! It's warm in here. You sure that forge isn't too hot?" and "Say, you sure have a lot of tools. Can you tell me the names of all of them?"

Freya elbowed Sif and whispered, "He's trying to distract the dwarfs. Get them to make three more gifts that *aren't* better than the ones Ivaldi's sons made."

"Yeah, so he gets the gifts we want, but they lose the bet!" Sif tapped palms with Freya in a silent high five.

However, Sindri wasn't having any of Loki's shenanigans. He soon banished the boygod through a white-painted door to wait in a windowless storage closet at the back of the workshop where he would be unable to talk to them *or* see what they were working on.

When Loki made a move to take with him the bag of gifts Ivaldi's sons had made, Sindri barked, "Leave 'em!

That way maybe you won't be tempted to weasel out of our deal and run off when you realize we're sure to win the bet!"

"Your lack of trust cuts me to the core," Loki replied. Still he left the bag on the floor of the workshop before disappearing into the storage closet.

"I take back that high five," Sif muttered to Freya as they crouched beneath the window. "Loki's *trying* to make things right, but I think he's going to need some help. I would feel awful if he lost his head finally doing a good deed."

"Then he shouldn't have made that stupid bet with them," Freya complained. But then she sighed. "Got a plan?" Though Loki might not be their favorite friend, neither girl wanted him to *die*. He could, too. He wasn't immortal, after all. None of the Norse goddesses and gods were. Though Idun's apples kept them all youthful, those apples couldn't prevent them from being killed.

"I do, actually," Sif said. It had come to her in a flash

as she watched Loki close himself into the storage closet. Quickly she explained her plan to Freya. Then the girls circled the workshop till they came to a blue door that led into that closet from the outside. They saw at once that the lock on the door was broken. Since Loki could easily escape through this door, Sindri had probably been wise to make him leave his bag of gifts inside the workshop. Loki wouldn't want to leave without those gifts.

"What are you doing here?" he asked in surprise when the girls opened the door.

They pushed past him to stand near some cupboards that stored blacksmithing supplies and tools. "We followed you from the Valhallateria," Sif admitted.

"You've been *spying* on me?" Loki asked, standing in the open doorway.

Ha! As if he never spied on others himself, thought Sif. This boygod was the king of spying!

"More like trying to make sure things go smoothly," Freya said coolly. Her fingers moved, automatically straightening the strings of the pouches dangling from her necklaces, as her restless fingers often did.

For a half second Loki's shoulders sagged and a worried look flitted across his face. Then he became his old cocky self again. "Butt out," he said bluntly. "I don't need help."

Sif raised an eyebrow at him. "Oh really? From what we've seen and heard so far, it seems like you're kind of in over your *head*. And *heading* for trouble." She bumped elbows with Freya and both girls grinned at her puns.

"Yeah," Freya went on, "so we wanted to give you a *heads*-up. To maybe stop any *heads* from rolling."

"Ha-ha." Unamused, Loki opened the door wider. He gestured toward it, saying, "So *not* sorry you have to leave. Bye now."

"Sure." Sif started for the door. "Too bad, 'cause we have a plan you could try. It involves shape-shifting. But since you don't want us to *bug* you with it . . ."

Catching on quickly, Freya followed her lead, adding,

"Then we'll just hope all goes well and *head* out. You've always had a good *head* on your shoulders. Good luck keeping it there."

Loki went pale. "Okay, okay," he said, swinging out an arm to stop them. "Let's not be hasty. What's your plan?"

By the time the girls finished explaining, Loki was grinning big and agreeing to their idea. "Now remember," Sif warned him before they left the storage closet, "only make the dwarfs cause *small* flaws."

"Right," Freya chimed in. "Just enough damage to help you win the bet. Nothing that will destroy the usefulness of the gifts."

"Got it," Loki assured them.

After dashing outside again, the girls rushed back to their previous vantage point at the side of the workshop. Through the window there they watched Sindri set a package of bacon (of all things!) and a lump of gold together in the forge.

"Now pump those bellows for all you're worth and don't stop till I say to," he instructed his brother. As Brokk began pumping air through the bellows to excite the fire and keep it roaring hot, Sindri waved his arms around in slow circles while reciting a magical chant:

"Take this lump that once was ore
And bacon that is pig no more."

Right in the middle of Sindri's chant, a fly buzzed out of the crack below the white door that led from the storage closet into the shop. The girls smiled at each other knowingly. Their plan had begun!

Zzzt! That fly zoomed around and around Brokk, who shook his head this way and that, trying to get it to buzz off. Annoying as the fly was, however, Brokk didn't once slow his pumping hands.

Meanwhile, Sindri finished his chant:

165

"Let my magic powers soar,

To create a golden boar."

With that, he reached into the forge with his tongs and pulled out a full-size boar made of gold with bristles that shone as bright as the sun.

The girls' eyes practically popped out of their heads. "Incredible!" Freya breathed in awe.

"Yeah, but it's flawless, so our plan isn't exactly working," said Sif. "Fly-Loki needs to annoy the dwarfs into making a few teeny mistakes in their gifts. Otherwise, their work will be better than the Ivaldi dwarfs', and he could be-*head*ing for deep trouble. If you know what I mean." She drew a finger across her throat to illustrate.

"Good work, bro," Sindri praised Brokk as the fly buzzed off to circle the room. "Two more gifts like this one and we'll have Loki's head decorating our shop for sure. Now keep those bellows going," he urged as he put another lump of gold in the forge.

Again Sindri waved his arms in circles and spoke:

> *"Listen to this chant I sing*
> *As I make my next great thing."*

He was only halfway through his chant when the fly was back to annoy Brokk again. *Zzzt! Zzzt!* This time it zoomed up his nose! Trying to dislodge the nostril invader, Brokk began huffing and puffing and snorting like a dragon. Suddenly he sneezed! *Ah-chooo!* Loki shot out of his nose like some kind of crazed winged booger!

Freya giggled softly. "Now this is more like it. Loki's doing a good job."

"Not *too* good, I hope," Sif said with a frown. "We don't want these dwarfs to mess up too badly. Then their gifts could turn out to be so crummy they're unusable."

Sindri had paused in the middle of this second chant

to glance in alarm at Brokk. But seeing that his brother had somehow managed to hold on to the bellows and keep pumping, he now finished the chant:

"From this lump of gold I'll bring
A magic arm-ring, fit for a king."

"Or a god," he added with a smile as he pulled a shining gold bracelet from the fire.

Sif and Freya exchanged a worried look. That bracelet looked perfect. So far Loki had been unable to cause even one tiny mistake. While Sif was wondering what kind of magic the beautiful bracelet contained, Sindri threw another lump of metal in the forge. Not gold this time, though. *Iron.* "Pump hard, brother," he encouraged Brokk. "You must not falter!"

As Brokk worked the bellows with all his muscled might, Sindri flung his arms in magical circles again and began to recite his third chant:

> *"Though in looks it may lack glamour,*
>
> *For this gift the gods will clamor."*

Zzzt! Zzzt! Fly-Loki had returned, landing right between Brokk's eyes and causing him to go momentarily cross-eyed. The dwarf's face scrunched and twitched as he tossed his head, trying to get rid of the fly. Thoroughly annoyed, Brokk stopped pumping for a beat to thrash out at the pesky insect. He missed, though. Fly-Loki was too fast for him and only began flying around and around him, doing crazy patterns in the air that caused the dwarf's eyes to spin.

"No matter what Loki does, Brokk just keeps those bellows going," said Sif. "This is not hurting Sindri's projects one bit."

Freya let out a huff. "This is Loki's last chance. I hate to say it, but things are not *head*ing in a good direction for him right now."

Sindri was glancing at his brother in alarm again, but he kept on chanting:

"'Woe is us,' the giants will yammer,

Cursing the day I created this . . ."

Zzzt! Zzzt! Sindri broke off his chant as the fly abruptly turned in midair and came at *him* instead. "Bug off!" He grabbed the tongs and swatted at it hard. *Whap!*

Fly-Loki fell to the floor! Sif and Freya looked at each other in horror. Had Loki met his end?

Phew! No! He'd only been stunned. Recovering a moment later, he half crawled and half buzzed off to the closet, where he disappeared under its door.

Just then Sindri pulled something from the forge. Whatever it was was so heavy that he couldn't lift it properly with his tongs and was forced to let the object drop to the floor. The girls craned their necks to see it.

"A hammer!" Freya exclaimed in a whisper. She was good at rhymes and often supplied rhyming words to complete the poems that Principal Odin was so fond of reciting.

Sif gave her two thumbs-ups, remembering Sindri's incomplete chant. "Of course! 'Hammer' rhymes with 'yammer,' 'clamor,' and 'glamour'!"

The iron hammer's head was the most massive Sif had ever seen—twice as long and wide as a loaf of bread! However, its handle was super short, possibly due to the missed beat of the bellows during fly-Loki's interference. Or maybe caused by Sindri's uncompleted rhyme. Either way, it seemed a flaw. Which meant their plan had worked! She only hoped the tool's usefulness was still intact.

"Sorry, bro. My bad," Brokk said sadly as he stared down at the hammer's handle.

"It was that stupid fly's fault, not yours," Sindri told him. "Besides, in the right hands—ones that can wield this hammer—it'll make a fine weapon. One that will thunder!"

Thunder? In the right hands? Considering his words, Sif smiled eagerly. Was it possible those "right hands"

Sindri had mentioned belonged to someone in their Thunder Girl pod? Maybe even *her*?

It sounded as if Sindri thought the hammer was still a success. Surely, its short-handle flaw would be enough to make Odin judge the first set of three gifts more highly than this second set, though!

"Tell Loki he can come out," Sindri told his brother. "Then go with him to Asgard to ask the gods for their judgment."

"Which will certainly be in our favor! We rocked it, bro!" said Brokk. The happy dwarfs each grabbed a set of tongs, held them high, and clanged them together in a blacksmithing high five.

Loki must have been listening at the white door, because he (in boy form now) popped out of the storage closet before Brokk could even start across the shop. Right away the boygod grabbed the bag containing the gifts Ivaldi's sons had made and slung it across one shoulder. "Time's a-wastin'," he said to Brokk cheerfully. "Gather up those gifts of yours and let's be off to the judging!"

From his merry tone it seemed obvious to Sif that Loki was convinced he'd win the bet. For his sake—or at least the sake of his poor *head*—she hoped he was right.

Brokk quickly bagged the golden boar and the bracelet. Then he and Sindri tugged and tugged at the massive iron hammer, trying to lift it from the floor. "Urgh. Oomph. Uh!" they cried out. It didn't budge. Not even an inch, resisting all of their efforts to move it. It was as if it were glued to the floor! Loki didn't even *try* to help them, but only watched with an amused look on his face.

"Never mind," Sindri said to Brokk at last. "I'll say a magic spell over it that will transport it to Asgard after you arrive." With that, Brokk and Loki made for the door of the workshop, each carrying a bag of gifts.

"Quick! We can't let Loki leave with my new hair!" Sif exclaimed to Freya. "The sooner I have it, the better for the wheat." The two girls left their hiding place at the side of the workshop and started around to the front.

Just as Sif and Freya rounded the corner of the workshop, they heard a loud *Caw! Caw!* Hugin and Munin were back! The girlgoddesses watched in astonishment as the ravens dove down from the sky. One of them caught the back of Brokk's shirt in its beak, and the other scooped up Loki in the same way.

"Wait!" Sif and Freya ran after them, shouting in unison. But Hugin and Munin paid them no heed and took to the skies with their burdens. Clamped in the birds' beaks and still clutching their bags of gifts, Loki and Brokk were carried off in the direction of Asgard.

"My hair!" wailed Sif.

"We'll get it," said Freya. "C'mon. Let's hurry back to school before the judging can begin!" Then and there, she pulled her cat's-eye marble from its pouch. After she summoned her cats, the girls leaped inside her red cart.

"Fly, kitty, kitty!" Freya commanded. They took off.

At Sif's request, Freya guided her cats to make a quick loop over Midgard's wheat fields before flying on to Asgard. The girls were horrified to see how withered and brown the fields looked. Freya shook her head. "Not good, is it?"

Sif twisted her hands together in her lap. "When I finally get my new hair, it's just *got* to work. The wheat must survive . . . and *thrive*."

"It will," Freya tried to reassure her. "I know it will."

Though encouraged by Freya's optimism, Sif was still worried. After all, could a metallic creation—however magical—really replace her amazing hair and bring back her goddess powers?

10
Judgment

THUMP! **THE CART BEARING THE TWO** girlgoddesses landed with a jolt in Asgard beside a short ramp leading down to the Bifrost Bridge. Sif and Freya jumped out. Snow had been falling while they were gone, and about a half foot of the powdery white stuff sparkled on the ground and frosted the trees. The second that Freya magicked her cart and cats into the cat's-eye marble and dropped it into its pouch, Skade and Idun popped out of the golden doors at the top of the bridge. Spotting Sif and Freya right away, the other two girls came thundering down the ramp toward them. *Clomp! Clomp!*

"I can't believe you two went off to Darkalfheim by yourselves. Without even telling us you were going!" Skade scolded immediately. She was wearing her newest pair of snow boots again, Sif noticed. The sparkly red ones.

"Odin sent us to meet you," Idun informed them in a gentler tone. She tucked a stray lock of her long brown hair under her yellow knitted hat. She'd stitched a big brown felt stem with a green felt leaf to the top of it, to make the hat resemble a gold-colored apple. "C'mon. All the teachers and students are assembling in Gladsheim Hall."

"Odin knows what Loki did to your hair, Sif," Idun went on as the four girls started up the ramp to the bridge. "And that you two followed Loki to Darkalfheim."

"And also what's happening to the crops in Midgard," Skade added.

"I imagine he knows a lot more than that," said Sif, thinking about the judging to come. It was probably on Odin's orders that Hugin and Munin had fetched Loki and Brokk and their gifts to Asgard!

"Hey, where's Heimdall?" Freya asked when they reached the double doors at the top end of the bridge. Asgard's sharp-eyed, keen-eared security guard wasn't at his usual post. Normally he stood on the bridge day and night, watching over it and guarding these golden portal doors, which served as magical shortcuts to Asgard and the academy halls within Yggdrasil's branches.

"Maybe he's up at Gladsheim already?" Skade wondered. Then she grinned. "Along with his noise-toot and hurt-stick." Heimdall liked to speak in kennings. His noise-toot was his horn, and his hurt-stick, his sword.

Holding hands so they would all stay together, the four girls leaped through the magical golden entrance to the academy. Seconds later they tumbled to a stop high in Yggdrasil's enormous, snow-covered branches.

Losing balance, Sif fell backward, pulling the other three girls down with her. But the snow made for a soft landing, and the girls only laughed. It was a welcome relief to laugh with friends after feeling so tense about her hair and everything lately. These girls always cheered her up, even when they weren't trying.

Up ahead Gladsheim Hall's silver-thatched roof shone in the sunshine that peeked between Yggdrasil's huge green leaves. Meeting in this location made sense, thought Sif, since it was AA's multipurpose gym/auditorium/assembly hall. After they were upright again, the girls made their way through the snow to the multipurpose hall's front doors. Along the way, Sif and Freya explained all that had happened at Darkalfheim to Skade and Idun.

Once inside Gladsheim, Sif was momentarily overcome with the usual admiration the hall inspired in her. Its walls shimmered and twinkled as if by magic because the paintings upon them contained tiny chips of glass that caught the light streaming in through the hall's windows. Most of these paintings were a tribute to Yggdrasil and the various animals the tree sheltered within its branches. Nidhogg the dragon's eyes glowed like rubies, the white spots on the deer glinted like ice, and Ratatosk the squirrel's fur sparkled. So beautiful!

Gladsheim was already jam-packed when the girls entered. It looked as if practically all of the academy's students and teachers were there. Across the room Sif spotted Odin. For a second his one good eye, the one without a black patch over it, seemed to fix on her. But then he looked away.

"Where's Thor?" Sif asked, but none of her friends knew.

"Heimdall's not here either," Idun commented in surprise.

"And what about Loki and Brokk?" Sif wondered aloud.

Freya shrugged. "I expected them to beat us here

too. But maybe the ravens were slowed down by all the weight they were carrying?"

The girls began to thread their way through the noisy crowd to the front of the room so they'd have a good view of what was to come. When students stopped Sif now and then to tell her how much they hoped Loki would make good on his promise to get the dwarfs to replace her hair, she thanked them.

It was warm and stuffy inside the crowded hall. After shucking off her cloak, Sif removed her knitted hat, too, and stuffed it into the pocket of her cloak. To her surprise, she was getting used to her short hair. Almost like it was starting to *grow* on her. Ha-ha! Still, that didn't excuse what Loki had done. Not at all.

"Fingers crossed your new hair restores your goddess powers," Skade murmured to her.

"Yeah. If I ever get it!" said Sif.

"You'd better!" Freya chimed in.

"Lives depend on it!" added Idun.

When they came even with Freya's brother, Frey, and some of his boygod friends, Frey said, "We heard Loki's on his way here with the gifts he promised. Any idea who'll get them?"

Relieved at this news, Sif replied, "There's a spear for Odin and hair for me. We don't know who the other gifts will go to."

"There are four more of them, right?" Bragi said eagerly. "I hope I get one."

"Me too!" called out several other students close enough to hear.

Sif sincerely hoped there'd be no arguments about who got those remaining gifts. Freya was probably thinking along the same lines, because she said to her brother and Bragi quickly, "Guess we'll just have to wait and see."

The four girlgoddesses continued past the boys till they were near the front of the crowd. From here they could easily see the two academy principals, Odin and Ms. Frigg, sitting side by side on carved wooden thrones that had been set up at the front of the room, facing the crowd. As usual, Ms. Frigg was knitting.

"Whee!" said a voice. The girls looked over to see that a corkscrew tubular fountain had begun bubbling up from the floor a dozen feet to one side of Odin. Bouncing like a ball atop its waterspout was the head librarian. Since he was supposed to be so supersmart, Sif wondered if Odin asked him here to help judge matters.

She craned her neck, studying the librarian. Something very weird and yellow was perched atop his bald head. "What's that thing Mimir's wearing? It's not his waterproof cap—that's orange and white."

"Looks like a scared cat with its fur sticking straight up," noted Skade.

"Actually, I think it's a toupee—you know, like a wig," Freya replied with a giggle.

Idun added, "Yeah, I saw him wearing it earlier

when I went looking for you guys in the library today. Gullveig said Mimir thinks it makes him look handsome."

Skade rolled her eyes. "If you ask me, his famed wisdom has failed him this time. Though I'd never tell *him* that."

Sif squinted at the clownish golden toupee a little harder. There was something so . . . *familiar* about it. Suddenly she did a double take. "Hey! He made that toupee from my *hair*! My old hair, I mean."

Her podmates stared at her in surprise. "It *is* the same color," Freya agreed slowly.

"But how did he get your—" Skade started to ask.

"I put my cutoff hair in a box and tossed it in a library trash can," Sif admitted before Skade could finish. "I didn't know what else to do with it, and its magic was gone."

"Well, Mimir seems to have recycled it," Freya said drily.

Sif glanced at the head librarian's toupee again. It looked so silly that she couldn't help giggling. "You're right."

"I bet Odin would be pleased if he knew that Mimir found a new use for your hair," said Freya. "He's been encouraging us to take care of the environment, after all. Finding new uses for stuff that would otherwise hit the trash is good for the World Tree!"

As if he'd heard them, Odin pivoted on his throne toward the four Thunder Girls. Fixing them with his good eye, he gave them a nod. A little surprised, the girlgoddesses still managed to nod back. He really did seem to know everything that went on around here. Sif had a feeling he knew and approved of her hair getting recycled!

Minutes later a hush stole over the hall as Hugin and Munin flew in with Loki, Brokk, and their bags. *Thunk! Thunk!* The birds deposited their heavy loads in front of the coprincipals. Then, uttering *Caw!*

Caw! the tired-looking ravens flew to Odin.

Mere seconds after they landed on his broad shoulders, a large object came hurtling through the air toward the front of the room. The *hammer*! Loki and Brokk barely had enough time to leap aside before it crashed onto the wooden floor in front of the thrones in the very place they'd just been standing, splintering the wood around it.

Odin laughed heartily. "Nothing much catches me by surprise, but *that* sure did!"

"Sorry," Brokk said, bobbing his head up and down. "My brother, Sindri, magicked it here because it was too heavy to pack in my bag."

Almost immediately students began to gather around the hammer, trying to lift it. One by one they failed.

"No harm done," roared Odin. "Except to the floor, of course. But that can be repaired." He paused for a moment as the raven on his right shoulder whispered something into his ear. "Yes, Hugin. You're quite right.

It *is* time for the judging to begin." The one-eyed principal rubbed his hands together, his gaze on the bags that Loki and Brokk held. "Okay, then. Who would like to go first?"

"Me!" Loki shouted. At once he began to brag about his visit to Darkalfheim and how he was able to use his cunning to secure "not one, not two, not three, but *six* gifts!" Loki could be charming, and his boasting seemed to amuse Odin. The principal's good eye twinkled as he smiled at the boygod.

Sif's friends, however, were less entertained. "How dare Loki take credit for *your* idea," Freya said to Sif indignantly.

Skade cupped her hands around her mouth. "The six gifts were Sif's idea, remember, Loki?" she called out. "That's how many she *told* you to bring back!"

Perhaps emboldened by Skade, Brokk poked a finger to Loki's chest and said scornfully, "Brag all you want now, boygod. But soon that clever tongue of yours won't be wagging." He made a slashing motion across his throat. "Just thinking a*head* to winning our bet!"

A murmur of confusion ran through the gleaming hall. Still, Loki looked cocky and unconcerned as he informed the crowd, "We made a bet about which set of gifts Odin will judge the finest! If Brokk and Sindri's gifts are judged superior to those made by Ivaldi's sons, I lose. And my head will roll!" he shouted out. "Literally!"

As his meaning sunk in, horrified gasps swept the crowd. Sure, Loki could be really annoying, but no one wanted to see him headless! The students quieted as the boygod opened the large bag he'd brought and took out the three gifts Ivaldi's sons had crafted.

Zing! Immediately the spear flew to Odin's hand. Loki grinned. "It seems the spear knows it was intended for you, Principal Odin," he said, turning toward Odin's throne. "Unlike other spears, it never misses its target."

Odin raised the spear and then sighted along its straight and true shaft. Nodding approvingly, he said, "Nicely done. I will call it Gungnir. It should serve me well in battle."

Next, Loki slipped the magical ship from its pouch and held it high for all to see. "When unfolded and set in the sea, this ship will grow big enough to hold an entire army. And as soon as its sail is hoisted, a wind will immediately fill it and blow the ship straight to its destination." As the crowd oohed and aahed, he added, "And once it has arrived at its destination, it can be folded back up and replaced in its pouch until the next time it's needed."

"Who's it for?" a boy demanded.

Abruptly the ship lifted from Loki. Rocking back and forth as if tossed by invisible waves, it skimmed a few feet over the heads of the crowd. Then it dropped down and landed on the head of Frey.

Though there were disappointed murmurs from

others who'd been hoping that the ship would be theirs, the crowd cheered for the well-liked boygod. Especially Freya, of course!

"I will name it *Skidbladnir*!" Frey announced, looking thrilled.

"My third gift," Loki said at last, "is the one I owe Sif." When she came forward to claim the metallic hair he held out to her, Loki looked sincere (for once) as he whispered, "Hope this makes up for what I did."

Though it wasn't an actual apology, Sif supposed it was the closest Loki could come to one, given his nature.

"Thanks," she whispered back. For a few seconds she fingered the golden hair. She was amazed at how fine its metallic strands were, so like her real hair had been, but with a golden gleam that was much brighter. As everyone watched, she placed the golden gift directly on top of her shorn locks.

The magic it was imbued with immediately took effect. Sif's eyes closed and her heart filled with joy as she felt the new hair binding seamlessly with her remaining stubble. And as it did so, she felt a sense of well-being and strength sweep over her. Which could only mean that her goddess powers had returned! Just to be sure, she opened her eyes and performed a quick test, shape-shifting into a swan. Score! It worked! The crowd erupted into applause as she rose to the ceiling and flew once around the room. What a wonderful feeling!

After retaking her girlgoddess form, Sif went to stand with her podmates. She hoped with all her heart that this restoration of her hair—and the powers that resided in it—hadn't come too late. If her new hair's powers were able to reverse the damage to the wheat crops in Midgard, there might yet be a good harvest. Especially if the giants who'd previously been stealing Midgard's wheat could be kept out of those fields from now on. *Hmm.* She eyed the hammer that still lay on the floor, knowing it could help with that effort.

Who would it choose? Maybe *her*? Or one of the other Thunder Girls?

"My turn now," Brokk said gruffly. After respectfully dipping his orange-fringed bald head in Odin and Ms. Frigg's direction, he opened his bag and took out one of the three gifts that he and Sindri had crafted.

"It may look simple, but it's not," he said as he held up the golden arm-ring. "Every nine days eight more gold rings just like the first will drop from it."

As his words died away, the bracelet flew to Odin. Looking pleased at receiving a second gift, Odin proclaimed that he would name the handsome gold bracelet Draupnir and slipped it over his arm.

Sif shifted her gaze to Loki. He had moved to a seat a short distance away on the platform that held Odin's and Ms. Frigg's thrones. He was frowning, she noticed. He had to be worried that Odin might favor Draupnir the bracelet over Gungnir the spear.

Next, Brokk drew out the golden boar. "I already

named him Gullinbursti. He can race faster than a horse and be ridden over land and sea and through the air. And since his bristles shine like the sun, nighttime riding is easy!"

Sighs of admiration and amazement swept the room. "Who's he for?" someone shouted out. It was a girl's voice this time.

Suddenly the boar made a grunting noise and shot through the crowd, which had no choice but to part for him. The boar stopped before Frey and nosed his hand. Seemed he'd gotten a second gift too!

"Why should Frey get *two* gifts?" Loki grumbled. Sif wondered if he'd hoped that one of the gifts would be for *him*. He didn't complain about Odin getting two gifts, though. Who would dare? She saw the dwarf send Loki a sly glance, seeming glad he was annoyed.

Before Brokk could present his final gift, the hammer that still lay on the splintered floor, there was a commotion at the back of the room near the door.

"Did we miss the judging?" Thor's voice boomed out as he and Heimdall strode into Gladsheim.

"Come!" Odin urged them. "You're just in time!" As Thor and the ten-foot-tall security guard made their way to the front of the room, Hugin and Munin left Odin's shoulders. The ravens flew over the top of the crowd before disappearing out the door that Thor and Heimdall had entered.

Sif barely had time to wonder where the birds were off to before Thor blurted out a report. "The giants are lurking on the second world ring, but no attacks anywhere yet!"

At this Odin began to explain to the crowd that Thor and Heimdall were late because he'd asked them to check on the protective border wall around Asgard. "Just wanted to make sure the frost giants weren't in a position to attack while we were all occupied here."

"What's this about?" Thor exclaimed when he

reached the front of the room and saw the hammer on top of the splintered floor. Various boygods and girl-goddesses were still trying to pick it up. So far it hadn't budged, despite dozens of student attempts.

Odin smiled. Then, as he sometimes did, he waxed poetic.

> *"A trifling accident.*
> *Nothing more.*
> *The hammer landed*
> *On the . . ."*

He paused, apparently unable to dredge up the right word.

Ms. Frigg looked up from her knitting. "Floor?" she supplied.

"Yes! That's the word I was looking for!" Odin agreed. His good eye was twinkling as he turned toward Brokk. "Does that hammer already have a name?"

Brokk dipped his head at Odin. "It's called Mjollnir."

"Mjollnir," Sif echoed quietly.

Freya leaned over and whispered, "Your runeword? That's a coincidence. Or maybe not?"

"Maybe not," Sif whispered back. She was half hoping the hammer would suddenly fly into her hands and claim her as its owner, but it didn't.

She watched Thor scratch his head. "Mjollnir? I've heard that name before," he said, sounding puzzled. Of course he had! She'd told him it was her runeword from class! "It's kind of in the way," he noted after a light-elf tripped over it. Bending low, he took hold of Mjollnir's short handle and easily swung the hammer up.

The crowd gasped as he then turned Mjollnir over and over in his big hands, examining it as if it were as light as a snowflake. Finally looking up, he noticed everyone's surprised faces. "What's the big deal?" he asked in confusion.

"It has chosen you," Brokk announced. "The gift, I mean."

Thor looked surprised. He tossed up the hammer end over end, then caught it again in one hand like it was nothing. "Okay. It's cool. But why is its handle so short?"

"Yes, why is that?" Loki asked Brokk, looking smug.

"No big deal. It's a small flaw," the dwarf said dismissively. He pinched the tip of his thumb and forefinger together to indicate just how small. With a nod toward Thor, Brokk said, "Despite the short handle, with this boygod's strength behind the hammer, it will be a huge help in guarding Asgard Academy against giants."

"An idle boast," Loki insisted hotly. "That hammer is obviously defective!"

Odin glanced over at Loki and frowned. Then he looked back at Brokk. "Tell me more about this hammer."

197

"Gladly," said Brokk. "Mjollnir is unbreakable. And no matter how far it is thrown, it will always return to its owner's hand."

Overhearing this claim, Thor tossed Mjollnir up to the ceiling. He'd misjudged his strength, however. The hammer tore through the ceiling's timbers and out through the roof. "Whoops," he said.

Lots of kids cracked up, including Loki. "Gladsheim just got a skylight," someone observed. Odin grinned, looking unperturbed by the damage.

Minutes passed. The hammer didn't return.

"Thanks, idiot. Looks like I win the bet," Loki said to Brokk. He had barely uttered those words when the hammer zoomed back to Thor's hand.

"Awesome!" Thor called out as he easily caught it. Then he began tossing it between his hands like a hot potato. "Ymir's beard! This thing gets red hot when it's thrown!"

"There's one more thing you should know about

Mjollnir," Brokk informed him. "If you ever need to hide it or carry it, it can magically shrink small enough to tuck inside your tunic pocket."

The already awestruck crowd murmured in wonder at what Mjollnir would be able to accomplish when wielded by the superstrong Thor. Loki didn't look at all thrilled to see him wind up with such a great gift, though.

"I should've guessed the hammer was meant for Thor," Sif whispered to Freya, who nodded back. He was, after all, the only one at the academy strong enough to handle it! "It's really a gift for all of Asgard!" Sif called out while looking at Loki. "A gift of protection against those who mean our worlds harm, and maybe even against Ragnarok in the future!"

"Whatever," Loki replied sullenly. Obviously, he wasn't convinced. Though Sif had kind of hoped the mighty hammer might've been intended for her or one of the other Thunder Girls, she had to admit that

Thor's hands were the right hands for Mjollnir.

A hush fell over the room as Odin stood up from his throne. Everyone wondered what his verdict regarding the winner would be. Which gifts would he judge best?

"I foresee that what this dwarf says about Mjollnir's attributes is true," he told the crowd. "And therefore, as wonderful as all these other treasures are, I judge Thor's hammer as the *most* valuable." With an apologetic glance in Loki's direction, he pronounced his judgment. "I declare Brokk to be the winner of the bet." With that, Odin plopped back down on his throne.

Brokk was beaming. "Then I lay claim to my prize—Loki's *head*!"

"Uh-oh," Sif whispered to Freya.

Choruses of "Oh no" filled the hall. Though most everyone likely thought it served Loki right to see the tables turned on him, no one wanted him to lose his head! At the same time, there was some laughter from a few who must've thought that Brokk couldn't be serious. She and Freya, however, *knew* that he was.

And so did Loki. His face went pale. "My head is of no use if it's not on my body," he protested.

"No worries," Odin said merrily. "Mimir manages fine. I can make sure you do too."

"Yeah, Loki," Mimir called out from his perch atop the fountain. "Once you wrap your *head* around the idea of being a no-body, it's great!"

"Hey, Loki," Thor boomed. "Just a *heads*-up that I'd like those yellow shoes of yours, since it's starting to look like you aren't going to need them anymore."

Loki's face turned red with anger and embarrassment. It looked like his head was going to explode before Brokk could even try to claim it. In typical Loki fashion, he tried to bargain with the dwarf. "How about if I give you its weight in gold, instead?"

"Ha!" Brokk replied, taking a determined step in his direction. "Why would I need your gold? Darkalfheim is rich in metals. I can get all the gold I want, whenever I want it."

Loki nodded his head slowly. *Possibly for the last time?* wondered Sif. "Well, then," he said at last. "I think maybe . . . I'll be off!" With that, he tried to race from the hall in his magic yellow shoes . . . only to find Thor, who could move surprisingly fast given how big he was, blocking the door.

While holding Mjollnir in one hand, Thor gripped Loki firmly with the other to keep him from shape-shifting his way out of this situation. "Seems to me you brought this down on your own *head*," he said as he marched Loki over to Brokk.

Now that she had new hair and her goddess powers were back, Sif was feeling generous. And sorry for Loki, too. She really didn't want to see him lose his head! But as it turned out, she needn't have worried.

"Hold on a minute." Loki backed away as Brokk unsheathed a wicked-looking knife that he'd taken from under his belt. A spark had come into the boygod's eyes, and it wasn't a spark of fear. A spark like that could mean only one thing, Sif thought. Loki had just come up with something clever!

Sure enough, he puffed out his chest and looked around at the assembled crowd to make sure they were watching him. "It's true that you are entitled to my head, Brokk," he said in a loud, theatrical voice.

"Glad you admit that," Brokk replied. He ran a finger lightly down his knife's blade, as if to test its sharpness. "Now if you'll come closer, I'll—"

"Here's the thing," said Loki. "Though I promised you my head, I didn't say you could have my ears or my nose or my eyeballs or my hair or my eyebrows or my neck."

"He's right!" Mimir piped up.

"B-but a head is no good without all that other stuff," Brokk argued with Loki. "It wouldn't make a good decoration at all!"

"Eww!" cried many students upon picturing the image his words called up. Many others were grinning or cracking up, though.

Odin, who had always had a special fondness for Loki despite his troublesome nature, guffawed and slapped his knee. "He's got you there, dwarf!" he called out to Brokk.

Realizing that Loki had truly outwitted the bloodthirsty dwarf, the crowd roared with laughter. Sif and her podmates joined in.

Loki grinned at Odin and then at his now-admiring audience. He even went so far as to take a bow.

Though he sheathed his knife, Brokk was too angry at losing his prize on a technicality to let the matter end there. "Well, since you didn't mention your clever mouth in your list," the dwarf told him, "at least I can shut it for a while. I'm sure everyone at Asgard Academy will appreciate that!" Quickly he chanted a spell:

"For one whole day
You'll zip your lip.
Nothing will you say.
Nothing will you sip."

A look of alarm came over Loki's face as he tried and tried to open his lips, but to no avail. It was as if they were glued shut.

"Now that's what I call being *tight-lipped*," Thor quipped, looking pleased at how things were turning out.

Odin leaned forward on his throne. If Loki had expected the principal to come to his rescue this time, he was sadly mistaken. Instead the principal fixed Loki with a steely gaze. Speaking sternly, he said, "In the future you will take more time to consider your actions"—and here he paused for a second and flicked Sif a look— "and think about who your true friends are."

Sif thought about Odin's words. By "actions" he seemed to be referring to Loki's cutting off her hair, plus

205

tricks he'd played on various other students in the past. And maybe even Loki's rash bet with Brokk.

But Odin had also implied that Loki didn't know who his "true friends" were. And that seemed to suggest Loki had *false* friends. Enemy giants perhaps, as many students suspected? If so, however, why had Loki gotten her hair and the other five gifts for Asgard? It was all so confusing. On the other hand, maybe it was just as confusing to Loki, who was, after all, *half*-giant. Maybe he truly didn't know whose side he was on!

As she was thinking all this over, caws rang out. With a flurry of flapping wings, Hugin and Munin appeared in the hall again. They soared over the heads of the crowd to land on Odin's shoulders. Then one of them whispered something in his ear that made him smile.

Leaping to his feet, he looked out over the crowd and announced, "You'll be pleased to know that with the restoration of Sif's hair, the wheat in Midgard grows tall and strong once more!"

All over the room cheers rang out. The four Thunder Girls hugged one another and hopped around with joy. So that was where Odin's ravens had gone, Sif realized. He must have sent them to check on the fields! Though relieved at his announcement, she was determined to go see for herself that the wheat crop was fine. But after such an eventful day she was bone-tired. The journey could wait till tomorrow morning.

Now that the show was over, the crowd began to shuffle out of Gladsheim Hall. As punishments went, Loki's zipped lips seemed like a fair one, Sif thought as she and her podmates made their way toward the door. Still, despite Odin's rebuke of the boygod's actions, she rather doubted that Loki would actually learn anything from it. She didn't need runes or a prophetic dream to predict that he'd be up to his usual tricks as soon as Brokk's spell wore off.

11
Lofn

"WATCH THIS," SIF TOLD SKADE, FREYA, AND Idun.

It was the next morning, and Sif stood in the middle of their podroom in Vingolf with the other three girl-goddesses gathered around her. While her podmates had slept in, she'd been experimenting with her new hair since the crack of dawn. She was excited to share what she'd discovered while practicing in front of a mirror, now that the others were finally awake.

"Curly," she instructed her metallic golden hair as she gave it a tap with her comb. Her friends gasped in delight as her hair magically corkscrewed itself into dozens of kinky coils upon command. "Not curly," she instructed, and it quickly went straight again.

"It can do other styles too," she told her podmates, before commanding her hair to weave itself into two, and then ten, braids. To amuse the others further, she made up some silly styles. "Rabbit ears," she ordered. Then, "Side buns." And finally, "Thunderbolt!"

The other three Thunder Girls cracked up as Sif's hair rose to form a jagged golden bolt atop her head. Skade was laughing so hard, she wound up rolling around down on the floor!

Sif just smiled. She loved that her new hair was not only super shiny and pretty, but also more magical than ever! Show over now, she returned her hair to the simple style she preferred—a ponytail.

"I know you guys are probably starving, but do

you think we could go to Midgard before breakfast?" she asked her friends once they'd calmed down. "I'm really anxious to see for myself that the wheat fields are healthy again."

"Yes! Let's go!" the other girls chorused. Since everyone was on board with the idea, they soon headed for the Bifrost Bridge. It was such a beautiful, sunshiny (though cold) day that they decided to walk to Midgard rather than fly in Freya's cart.

"Where are you Thunder Girls off to this morning?" Heimdall greeted them when they came through the golden portal doors to start down the bridge. Dressed in his official-looking uniform, the super-tall, broad-shouldered, and muscular security guard could be quite intimidating when he needed to be. The enormous sword (aka hurt-stick) strapped to his side made him appear even more fearsome. Sif had been a little afraid of him when she'd first come to AA. But not anymore.

Heimdall stroked his long, pointy beard, frowning slightly as she explained that they were heading for Midgard to check on the wheat crop. "Watch out for trolls under the bridge. And lurking giants on the second ring," he cautioned the girls sternly, before stepping aside so they could pass. At all times watchful and on the alert, he was actually kind of a worrywart. He probably wouldn't have allowed any student to leave the safety of Asgard—*ever*—if it had been up to him.

"If we see any trolls, we'll give 'em a good kick with our thunder boots," joked Skade. She lifted her foot to show him that she was wearing her sturdiest and thickest-soled pair of hiking boots.

Heimdall grunted. But then, he was known for his sharp eyes and keen ears, *not* for his sense of humor.

In high spirits, the four girls clomped down the bridge, laughing and chatting. But as they drew closer to Midgard, they slowed their steps and grew quiet. Sif wondered if, like her, the others were also a little worried that all might not be well, despite what the ravens had told Odin last night.

Suddenly they came to a spot on the bridge that overlooked the Midgard fields. There they stood in awe, for spread out before them were great, gleaming fields of wheat. For miles around the grain stood tall and straight again, all signs of withering erased.

"Hooray!" Sif exclaimed, happily jumping around. The other girls punched fists in the air and whooped so loudly that their voices echoed into the valleys. As if in response to the thunderous, joyful sound, a breeze whipped across the fields right then, making the wheat ripple in such a way that it appeared to be waving to them in thanks.

"You're welcome!" shouted Sif. At this they all giggled. After their joyous whoops subsided, they stood on the bridge for several long moments, surveying the golden fields and feeling happy. Then, with great gladness in their hearts, they turned and headed back toward the academy.

After just a few minutes, they came to the small off-ramp that led to the Midgard Mall. "Hey! We should stop at the mall. The boot sale is still going on!" Skade informed the others.

Her three podmates laughed. But then Sif said, "Well, why not?" So the four girlgoddesses thundered down the ramp and into an enormous, fancy wooden building. It was divided into many spacious and well-lit stalls that housed the various shops within. The girls were admiring the display in a boot shop window when another window display one stall over caught Sif's eye. She ducked inside the shop, which was called Mighty Mitts and Knits, and made a quick purchase. Then she and Freya waited outside a snack shop called Sweet Eats while Idun and Skade went inside to get scones for the trip home.

While she and Freya were waiting, Sif glanced at the

other shoppers going by and was startled to find herself abruptly gazing into a familiar face among them. A girl with short-cropped black hair. Lofn! Both girls instantly looked away without speaking.

"Of all people," murmured Sif. Lofn, her former BFF, had appeared just as upset and startled to see *her*.

"What's wrong?" asked Freya.

Frustration rose in Sif as she glanced over at Lofn again and saw her scurry toward the mall's exit door. Pointing her out to Freya, Sif blurted out, "See that girl? Her name's Lofn, and, well, we used to be friends."

"Used to be?" Freya asked as the girl disappeared through the door.

"Back in our village in elementary school," said Sif. "Second grade."

"So what happened to change things?" Freya asked.

Sif hesitated for a few moments, but then, overcoming her reluctance to talk about it, she plunged ahead with her story in a rush. "Speaking up in class was always scary for Lofn. She never asked questions or volunteered answers." After a slight pause, she added, "I had my own difficulties, though. Reading was hard for me. Still is, actually."

"I didn't know that," said Skade. She and Idun had come out with scones and had overheard. As the girls left the mall, Idun handed out the scones. Sif didn't take one, however. She needed both hands to carry her Mighty Mitts and Knits bag. Plus, seeing Lofn had taken away her appetite.

The four girls went up the ramp to rejoin the Bifrost Bridge. As her podmates walked along munching their scones, Freya encouraged Sif to go on with her story. "So Lofn and I bonded over our problems," Sif told them. "She helped me with my reading, and I spoke *for* her in class."

Skade lifted an eyebrow. "And your teacher let you do that?"

Sif shrugged. "Most of the time. But then we were

assigned this big oral report. And the teacher said it was an *individual* report. That we couldn't do it together. Lofn was so worried about it that she got a stomachache the day before."

"I know the feeling," admitted shy Idun.

"I decided to use my prophetic abilities to help her," Sif continued. "I was getting pretty good at rune writing by then and feeling a little too confident. So when Lofn went to see the school nurse, I found a soft piece of wood in the forest at recess and carved the rune symbols for the word *bitr* into it with a sharp rock."

Skade interrupted Sif's story to say, "*Bitr* as in 'brave,' right?"

Sif nodded. "Anyway, I dropped the rune-charm into Lofn's schoolbag, hoping it would magically give her courage when it was time to deliver her report."

"But something went wrong," Freya guessed.

Feeling unsettled by memories, Sif sighed and shifted her bag from one hand to the other as they walked ever upward. They were nearing Asgard now. Farms and villages dotted the landscape below, and up above they were beginning to catch glimpses within Yggdrasil's branches of the roofs of various halls.

"Lofn didn't show up for school the next morning. She'd gotten really sick overnight, with a fever and a horrible rash. Luckily, her doctor was also a master of runes. Right away he suspected magic as the cause of her illness. So he searched and found the rune-charm I'd put into Lofn's bag."

"So your charm made her sick?" Idun asked.

"Bingo. I'd made a huge mistake," Sif admitted. "Instead of the word *bitr*, I mixed up my symbols and carved the word *eitr*."

Her three podmates gasped. *"Poison!"* exclaimed Freya.

"Uh-huh," said Sif, nodding. "After the doctor burned the charm, Lofn got better. Her parents wouldn't let us hang out after that, though. They couldn't forgive me. And the thing is, I've never forgiven myself either. Plus, Lofn won't even look at me. She pretty much hates me, I think."

"That's so sad," Idun said.

"Yeah, you only meant to help," Skade said soothingly.

Freya reached over and gave Sif's shoulders a quick squeeze. "Your heart was in the right place. Remember what Ms. Frigg is always saying, that prophecy is more an art than a science, with more opportunity for error."

"But mistakes like the one I made with Lofn make being a seer feel like a big fat burden," Sif said softly.

"I know what you mean," Freya told her. "But seeing is a gift, and you're good at it!"

Her kind words made Sif smile a little. Though things were still the same between Lofn and her, she felt surprisingly better for finally having gotten the

Horrible Thing off her chest. These girls obviously liked her *despite* her failings. In fact, it led them to admit their own.

"Nobody's perfect," Skade said. "I can be a little messy, for instance."

The others laughed. Rolling her eyes, Freya said in mock surprise, "No, really?"

"I can get a little apple-obsessed and forget promises or appointments," said Idun.

They all looked at Freya, expecting her to admit some failing too. She looked around the group. "What? I'm perfect!" she exclaimed. Then she laughed. "Just kidding. Frey thinks I'm jewelry- and fashion-obsessed, but what's not to like about those things?" She gestured toward the many necklaces she was wearing, as well as her stylish embroidered *hangerock* with its beautiful flower and leaf design. This cracked them all up again.

Sharing these things made Sif feel even closer to these girls. It was a feeling she liked a lot. Friendship itself was a gift, yet these girlgoddesses had just given her another gift. A renewed belief in herself as a seer. She would have to work harder than some to overcome her rune-reading difficulties, but maybe she could do it, with the support of her friends.

They'd reached the Asgard end of the bridge by now, and Heimdall stepped up to greet them. "All A-OK in the wheat fields?" he asked, looking at Sif.

"The crops are tops," she answered with a smile.

At this, Heimdall gave her one of his rare grins, showing off blinding-gold teeth that matched the shine of the double doors. "Where to now, Thunder Girls?" he asked.

Skade looked around at the others. "Want to get breakfast at the V? I'm still hungry."

Freya and Idun nodded in agreement.

"Me too," said Sif. She hadn't felt like eating before,

but after unloading all that stuff from her past and talking about being a seer, she now felt lighter. And hungrier!

Pointing his hurt-stick toward the golden portal doors, Heimdall boomed out, "THUNDER ON, GIRLS!"

12
One Last Gift

As **soon as the four girlgoddesses**

entered the portal, they were whisked away. When

they tumbled to a stop, they were only a short distance

from the Valhallateria. Sif, Freya, Skade, and Idun were

almost ready to head inside when Thor strode toward

them from the direction of the border wall. Guard duty

again, Sif supposed.

"Hey, Sif, wait up!" he called to her.

She set her heavy bag on the snow-covered ground

between her boots and looked at her friends. "Go on in. I'll catch up with you in a few." At this, Freya smiled that maddeningly knowing smile of hers, but she said nothing about crushing, thank goodness.

"Okay. Later," said Idun as she, Skade, and Freya pushed through the V's doors.

With his superlong strides, Thor reached Sif in no time at all. Mjollnir was hanging from his Belt-o'-Power, she noted. "So how's the hammer working out for you?" she asked.

"I scared off three frost giants with it just this morning," he informed her proudly. "It works great but is a bit tricky to use, since the handle's so short. Like I said during the judging, it gets superhot when I throw it. Singes my fingers every time it flies back to me."

"Oh! That reminds me." Quickly she handed him the heavy bag containing the purchase she'd made at the mall.

The superstrong boygod lifted the bag as if it

weighed no more than one of Sif's hair ribbons. Seeing the Mighty Mitts and Knits logo on it, he asked dubiously, "What's this? It's not from Ms. Frigg, is it?"

Sif grinned. He probably feared the bag contained one of Ms. Frigg's misshapen hats. "No. It's a small gift. From me."

Already looking pleased, Thor opened the bag. A puzzled look came over his face as he pulled out two heavy iron gloves. But then realization dawned and his face lit up. "For catching Mjollnir?" he guessed.

She smiled, nodding. "They seemed thick enough to protect your hands and keep them from getting too hot. Almost like armor."

"Genius idea!" Thor exclaimed. He tried on the heavy gloves. "A perfect fit! Thanks. I really like you . . . uh . . . I mean your *new hair*!" His face turned redder than Skade's sparkly red boots. Looking alarmed and embarrassed, he spluttered, "I mean, I really like the *gloves*!"

"I'm glad," she said, grinning. She liked him, too. As

a friend, anyway. As far as crushing went . . . well . . . time would tell.

Instead of taking off the gloves, he kept them on, turning his hands this way and that to admire them as they went inside. Ever the gentleman, he held open the door with one gloved hand.

"I wonder how Loki's doing?" she asked after a glimpse around the room showed that he wasn't there. "He must be getting really hungry by now, since he can't eat with his lips sealed."

"He'll survive. Brokk's spell will wear off by dinnertime. Unfortunately." Thor's face brightened. "In the meantime, everyone can enjoy a break from his yapping and trickery. I know I will!"

Sif laughed. A moment later they parted as their friends waved them over to different tables. She had just sat down between Idun and Skade when a Valkyrie fluttered by with a breakfast tray and offered her a plate of sausages with freshly baked bread and cheese. After she took it, the Valkyrie flew off to deliver more plates of food. Sif was about to tuck into her breakfast when she heard a squirrelly voice calling her name. Ratatosk! What did he want?

"Message from Odin," the large squirrel called out. He scampered to sit on her table, where he pulled an acorn from his knapsack Not an ordinary acorn, but a message acorn, which could *speak*.

When he tossed the special acorn to Sif, she caught it. No need to ask *how* Odin knew where she was. From Hlidskjalf, his high seat in Valaskjalf Hall, he could see everything that happened in all nine worlds!

"Thanks," she told Ratatosk as she opened her hand to gaze at the acorn. It was adorable with its cute face and hat! What could Odin want to say to her, though? she wondered anxiously. She hoped she and Freya weren't in hot water for having gone to Darkalfheim yesterday without telling anyone they were leaving.

Instead of going off to deliver more messages, the gossipy squirrel made himself at home. After tying a napkin around his neck, he sat cross-legged on the table and began helping himself to leftovers from the other three girls' plates. By sticking around, the busybody squirrel was probably hoping to hear some delectable piece of gossip from the acorn that he could then spread.

The message acorn boinged up and down a few times in the palm of Sif's hand, each boing carrying it higher. "Happy, happy, thank you!" it said in its babyish singsongy voice.

"Who's happy and thanking me? Odin?" Sif asked, as Freya, Idun, Skade, and Ratatosk looked on.

"Yes, silly!" said the nutty little acorn, doing a somersault. (Message acorn vocabularies were seriously limited.)

When it failed to say more, Sif tapped a fingertip on its tiny hat. "*Why* is Odin happy and thanking me?"

227

The message acorn did a twirl, then smiled up at her. "Gifts!"

Skade took a sip from her *hrimkalder*, then set it down. "Sweet!"

"The apple juice, you mean?" asked Idun, confused.

"Well, that too. But I meant it's sweet that Odin sent an official thanks to Sif for the gifts she made Loki bring to AA," Skade explained. "I wasn't sure he heard my shout-out about that last night in Gladsheim, but he must have."

"Sweet! Righty-o!" squealed the acorn. Finished with its message, it bounced off Sif's hand and rolled away across the floor.

Ratatosk tossed off his napkin and scrambled after the acorn. Once he'd retrieved it, he stuck it back in his knapsack before going out the door. Apparently, message acorns were reusable!

After some gentle teasing about her being Odin's pet

and also about Thor's interest in her, Sif's friends moved on to other topics. As they chatted, Sif finished her breakfast, thinking that it was cool and "sweet" indeed that Odin had been pleased enough with her part in the gift-getting to send her a special thanks.

The last few days had been full of highs and lows. But despite the trauma of losing her hair and seeing Midgard's wheat crop come perilously close to being destroyed, things were better than ever now! And the dwarfs' other gifts—especially Mjollnir—would help keep the giants (and Ragnarok) at bay for the time being. To think that she'd *foreseen* these gifts!

Remembering Freya's kind words about her seeing skills, Sif found herself more determined than ever to learn as much as she could to improve her talent. Glancing around the table at the smiling faces of Freya, Skade, and Idun, she realized that her strengthened friendships with them and Thor were the absolute best thing to have happened in the last few days. Because as powerful as goddess magic could be, friendships were even *more* powerful!

From the corner of her eye she glimpsed Lofn heading over to the goat fountain for apple juice. Hmm . . . speaking of friendships . . . did she dare? Would Lofn rebuff her if she tried to speak to her? That would be embarrassing, but she had to try. Before she could lose her courage, Sif leaped up and went over to the fountain too.

Lofn nearly dropped the green glass cup she was holding under one of Heidrun's many spigots when she looked up and saw Sif standing next to her. "Oh! Sorry," said Sif. "I didn't mean to startle you." She took one of the *hrimkalders* from the table and held it under a spigot too, just to have something to do. "Isn't this the best juice ever?" she went on, though Lofn hadn't said a word.

Lofn nodded, still silent. But at least she didn't leave.

Sif took a deep breath. "I didn't do it on purpose."

Lofn shot her a quick look but didn't speak.

"I mean, I feel horrible about what happened back in the village," Sif continued.

"Me too!" Lofn finally blurted out, breaking her silence at last.

"Really?" Happiness overflowed in Sif at the same time apple juice overflowed her cup. *Oops.* She pulled it away from the ever-flowing spigot. "But why should *you* feel horrible about what happened? It was my fault you got sick. I should have been more careful!"

Lofn shook her head. "I always knew it was an accident. We were only little kids. You were trying to help me. I feel bad that I didn't try harder to make my parents understand. It was easier to go along with their decision to keep us apart. I'm sorry."

"Trying to convince them to change their minds wouldn't have been easy," Sif protested. "After all, you were only a little . . ."

"Kid," they both finished. They laughed about using the same line. And because they were standing at a *goat* fountain.

"We're not little kids anymore," Sif pointed out.

Lofn smiled. "No. And I can make my own decisions about who my friends will be now." Her voice turned soft and hopeful. "Friends again?"

"Yes!" said Sif, grinning wide. Just as apple juice had overflowed her cup, happiness now overflowed *her*.

"Oh no!" Lofn cried in alarm.

"What?" asked Sif, equally alarmed. Had Lofn already changed her mind about being friends? But when a peach flew by Sif's ear, she whipped around and realized what was going on. Warriors inside the carved friezes had sprung into action. Their usual end-of-meal battle was on!

"Food fight!" she and Lofn said at the same time.

Grinning at each other, the two new old friends ducked just in time to avoid a wedge of cheese that

 232

came hurtling toward them. Giggling, with *hrimkalder* in hand, they dove beneath the table where the fountain sat. There they would have tons to talk about while they waited the fight out, friends once more!

Authors' Note

To WRITE EACH BOOK IN THE THUNDER GIRLS series, we choose one or more Norse myths and then give them an updated middle-grade twist. After deciding on what elements we'll include from various retellings of the myths, we freely add interesting and funny details in order to create meaningful and entertaining stories we hope you'll enjoy.

We also write the Goddess Girls middle-grade

series, which features Greek mythology. So why write another kind of mythology now too? Good question! Our enthusiasm for Norse mythology strengthened after Suzanne began frequent visits to her daughter and granddaughter, who live in Oslo, Norway. There, representations of the Norse gods and goddesses and their myths are found in many museums. Along the walls in the courtyard of the Oslo City Hall, there are painted wooden friezes (by painter and sculptor Dagfin Werenskiold) that illustrate motifs from various Norse myths. These friezes are the inspiration for the Valhallateria friezes that come alive at the end of meals in Thunder Girls!

We hope our series will motivate you to seek out actual retellings of Norse myths, which will also give you more understanding of and "inside information" about characters, myths, and details we've woven into Thunder Girls. Below are some of the sources we consult to create our stories.

- *D'Aulaires' Book of Norse Myths* by Ingri and Edgar Parin D'Aulaire (for young readers)
- *The Norse Myths* by Kevin Crossley-Holland
- *The Prose Edda* by Snorri Sturluson
- *The Poetic Edda* translated and edited by Jackson Crawford
- *Norse Mythology: A Guide to the Gods, Heroes, Rituals, and Beliefs* by John Lindow
- *Norse Mythology A to Z* by Kathleen N. Daly

For more about the art and friezes at Oslo City Hall, visit theoslobook.no/2016/09/03/oslo-city-hall.

Happy reading!

Joan and Suzanne

Acknowledgments

Many thanks to our publisher, Aladdin/Simon & Schuster, and our editor, Alyson Heller, who gave an immediate and supportive yes to our idea to write a Norse mythology–based middle-grade series. Alyson edits both Goddess Girls and Heroes in Training, our ongoing Greek mythology–based series for children. We have worked with her for many years and feel very lucky to be doing another new series with her and the other fine folk at Aladdin.

They help make our words shine, design fabulous art to make our books stand out, and make every effort to see that our books reach as many readers as possible.

We are also indebted to our literary agent, Liza Voges. She has championed us in all our joint series ventures and worked hard on our behalf and on behalf of our books. Thank you, Liza!

We are grateful to Danish artist Pernille Ørum for her striking jackets for these books in our Thunder Girls series, and we look forward to more of her cover art.

Finally, we thank our husbands, George Hallowell and Mark Williams, for offering advice when asked, troubleshooting computer problems, and just making our lives richer and easier. During hectic times in our writing schedules they're always good sports, taking up the slack of daily chores without complaint.

Glossary

NOTE: PARENTHESES INCLUDE INFORMATION specific to the Thunder Girls series.

Aesir: Norse goddesses and gods who live in Asgard

Alfheim: World on the first (top) ring where light-elves live

Alfrigg: One of Ivaldi's sons, the dwarf blacksmiths who help craft Sif's new hair, Odin's spear, and Frey's ship

Amma: Means "grandmother" (nickname for Gullveig)

Angerboda: Loki's giantess wife whose name means "distress-bringer" (angry Asgard Academy student and girlgiant)

Asgard: World on the first (top) ring where Aesir goddesses and gods live

Berling: One of Ivaldi's sons, the dwarf blacksmiths who help craft Sif's new hair, Odin's spear, and Frey's ship

Bifrost Bridge: Red, blue, and green rainbow bridge built by the Aesir from fire, air, and water

Bragi: God of poetry (student at Asgard Academy and boygod)

Breidablik Hall: Hall of the Norse god Balder (boys' dorm at Asgard Academy)

Brising: Freya's necklace, shortened from *Brísingamen* (Freya's magic jewel)

Brokk: Dwarf blacksmith who works with his brother, Sindri, in Darkalfheim

Darkalfheim: World on the second (middle) ring where dwarfs live

Draupnir: Magical golden arm-ring that the dwarfs Brokk and Sindri make as a gift for Odin

Dvalin: One of Ivaldi's sons, the dwarf blacksmiths who help craft Sif's new hair, Odin's spear, and Frey's ship

Dwarfs: Short blacksmiths in Darkalfheim (some young dwarfs attend Asgard Academy)

Fensalir Hall: Hall of the Norse goddess Frigg (hall where she teaches fourth-period Runes class)

Frey: Vanir god of agriculture and fertility whose name is sometimes spelled Freyr, brother of Freya (Freya's twin brother and Asgard Academy student and boygod)

Freya: Vanir goddess of love and fertility (Vanir girlgoddess of love and beauty who is an Asgard Academy student)

Frigg: Goddess of marriage, who is Odin's wife (coprincipal of Asgard Academy with Odin)

Fire giants: Terrifying giants who live in Muspelheim

Frost giants: Descendants of Ymir from Jotunheim

Gladsheim Hall: Sanctuary where twelve Norse gods hold meetings (Asgard Academy's assembly hall)

Grerr: One of Ivaldi's sons, the dwarf blacksmiths who help craft Sif's new hair, Odin's spear, and Frey's ship

Gullinbursti: Magical golden boar that the dwarfs make as a gift for Frey

Gullveig: Vanir sorceress whose gold-hunting in Asgard causes the Aesir-Vanir war (Freya and Frey's nanny and library assistant at the Heartwood Library)

Gungnir: Magical spear that the dwarfs make as a gift for Odin

Hangerock: Sleeveless apronlike dress, with shoulder straps that are fastened in front by clasps, that is worn over a long-sleeved linen shift

Heidrun: Goat that produces mead for the fallen warriors in Valhalla (the ceramic goat fountain in the Valhallateria)

Heimdall: Watchman of the gods (security guard at Asgard Academy)

Helheim: World on the third (bottom) ring inhabited by the evil dead and ruled by a female monster named Hel

Hlidskjalf: Odin's throne

Hugin: One of Odin's two ravens whose name means "thought"

Idun: Aesir goddess who is the keeper of the golden apples of youth (Asgard Academy student and girl-goddess)

Ivaldi's Sons: Four dwarf blacksmiths who craft three gifts for the gods, including Sif's new hair

Jotun: Norse word for "giant"

Jotunheim: World on the second (middle) ring where frost giants live

Kenning: Nickname made up of two descriptive words connected by a hyphen

Kvasir: Vanir god sent to Asgard at the end of the Aesir-Vanir war who offered helpful information (Asgard Academy student and boygod from Vanaheim)

Light-elves: Happy Asgard Academy students from Alfheim

Loki: Troublemaking, shape-shifting god of fire (Asgard Academy student and boygod)

Midgard: World on the second (middle) ring where humans live

Mimir: Wise Aesir god who was beheaded and revived by Odin ("head" librarian at Asgard Academy)

Mimir's Well: Well of wisdom at the end of Yggdrasil's second root in Jotunheim

Munin: One of Odin's two ravens whose name means "memory"

Muspelheim: World on the third (bottom) ring where fire giants live

Nerthus: Freya and Frey's mother, a peace-bringing earth goddess who drives a cart pulled by cows

Nidhogg: Dragon that lives in Niflheim and gnaws at the root of the World Tree

Niflheim: World on the third (bottom) ring where the good dead are sent

Njord: Vanir god of the sea sent to Asgard after the Aesir-Vanir war (Asgard Academy student and boygod from Vanaheim)

Norse: Related to the ancient people of Scandinavia, a region in Northern Europe that includes Denmark, Norway, and Sweden and sometimes Finland, Iceland, and the Faroe Islands

Od: Norse god who is Freya's lost husband (Asgard Academy student and boygod who tends to get lost)

Odin: Powerful Norse god of war, wisdom, and poetry who watches over all nine worlds (coprincipal of Asgard Academy with his wife, Ms. Frigg)

Parhalling: Norwegian folk dance

Ragnarok: Prophesied doomsday when goddesses and gods will fight a fiery battle against evil that could destroy all nine Norse worlds

Ratatosk: Squirrel that runs up and down Yggdrasil spreading gossip and insults

Runes: Ancient, magical Norse symbols carved in wood, stone, or metal and used like alphabet letters to form words

Sif: Golden-haired goddess of the harvest (Asgard Academy student and girlgoddess)

Sindri: Dwarf blacksmith who works with his brother, Brokk, in Darkalfheim

Skade: Goddess of skiing, sometimes spelled Skadi (Asgard Academy student and half-giant girl)

Skidbladnir: Magical ship that Ivaldi's sons made as a gift for Frey

Spring of Mimir: Water spring on the second (middle) ring of the Norse world whose waters feed Yggdrasil

Tanngnjóstr: "Teeth grinder," one of Thor's two goats

Tanngrisnir: "Teeth barer," one of Thor's two goats

Thor: Superstrong Norse god of thunder and storms (Asgard Academy student and boygod)

Trolls: Subgroup of giants who live in Ironwood Forest near Midgard (barefoot troublemakers at Bifrost Bridge)

Valhalla: Huge room in Asgard where dead warriors feast and fight (Valhallateria, Asgard Academy's cafeteria)

Valkyries: Warrior maidens in winged helmets who choose which warriors will die in battle and then bring them to Valhalla (cafeteria ladies and workers in Asgard Academy's Valhallateria)

Vanaheim: World on the first (top) ring where Vanir goddesses and gods live

Vanir: Norse goddesses and gods that live in Vanaheim

Vingolf Hall: Goddesses' meeting hall at Asgard (girls' dorm at Asgard Academy)

Well of Urd: Water spring on the first (top) ring of the Norse world whose waters feed Yggdrasil (a meeting place for Odin and Mimir)

Yggdrasil: Enormous ash tree that links all nine ancient Norse worlds, also called the World Tree (location of Asgard Academy)

Ymir: Very first frost giant whose body parts were used to create the Norse cosmos, including mountains, the sea, and the heavens

Don't miss the next book in
the Thunder Girls series!

TWELVE-YEAR-OLD IDUN AND HER FRIENDS, Freya, Sif, and Skade, stomped the snow from their boots as they entered Midgard Mall. "Want to split up to shop at different stores and then meet back here later?" Idun asked the others.

The four girlgoddesses had only just become friends a few weeks ago when they'd all begun attending Asgard Academy and been thrown together as roommates. Principal Odin had invited (ordered, actually) students from all nine worlds of the Norse universe—located on three enormous ring-shaped levels stacked one above the other—to enroll at the newly formed academy.

Skade nodded. "Good idea. I want to check out the boot sales." A half-giant from a second-level world called Jotunheim, she was crazy about boots. The pros and cons of various ski, snow, or high-fashion ones were all Skade had talked about as the girls had walked down the Bifrost Bridge to get to the mall. That tri-color red, blue, and green bridge connected this second-level world of Midgard with the first-level world of Asgard, which was where their academy was located.

"Maybe I'll go with you," Sif told Idun. Sif's golden hair, which wasn't real but had been spun from metallic gold threads by two talented dwarfs, shone brightly in the rays of sun filtering through a skylight overhead. "Just to look, though. I've already got two pairs of boots, so I don't really need new ones."

Skade gave her head a shake to dislodge snowflakes.

The motion sent her long, white-streaked black hair swaying from side to side. "Need schmeed. You can *never* have too many boots!"

The other girls laughed. After they all agreed to meet back at the entrance in an hour, Idun whipped out four small snack bags. "Hey, before we split up . . . I brought dried apple chips for everybody."

"Oh, thanks," said Freya, tucking the bag Idun handed her into her pocket.

"Yeah," murmured Skade, quickly pocketing hers, too.

"So thoughtful of you," Sif added a little too brightly. In fact, as Idun began munching her apple chips (*mmm, nice and chewy*), she noticed that she was the only one doing so.

"Aren't you hungry?" she asked Freya after Skade and Sif headed off.

"I'm saving my chips for later," Freya replied as the two girls started to walk. But Idun noticed her smile seemed a little forced.

Her friends' lack of enthusiasm for the apple chips

she'd brought along left Idun feeling a little bummed. She was the goddess of youth, and her magical and deliciously sweet golden apples were what kept all of the academy's goddesses and gods healthy and youthful. Didn't her friends appreciate that?

"So what did you want to shop for? I'm thinking clothes," Freya said, changing the subject. "Although I need more of those like Skade needs more boots!" she added.

Setting aside her hurt feelings, Idun smiled. They both knew Freya already had way more clothes than would fit in her wardrobe back at their room in the girls' dorm. Freya was the most fashion-forward girl at the academy. Though all the girls wore sleeveless wool dresses called *hangerocks* over their simple white linen shifts, hers were always the cutest!

"Skade says you can never have too many boots. Maybe the same could be said about clothes," said Idun. *And apple chips,* she thought, but didn't say. "I love your *hangerock* by the way."

"Thanks! I made it myself." Freya did a quick pose to better display the dark blue *hangerock* she wore beneath her red wool cloak. White snowflakes embroidered around the *hangerock*'s hem sparkled, and its shoulder straps fastened at the front with fancy tortoiseshell clasps. Small leather pouches containing intriguing objects dangled from nine bead, seed, or chain necklaces strung between these clasps in a big swoopy smile-shape swag across Freya's chest.

"Everybody sews where I'm from in Vanaheim," Freya went on. "But that doesn't mean I don't like shopping for something someone else made for a change. Plus, sometimes it gives me sewing ideas."

As they walked on, Idun gazed ahead to the rows of stores. "I wonder where we should start?" she murmured, munching her chips. They were delicious *and* nutritious. It made no sense that her friends hadn't gobbled them up right away. After all, they hadn't eaten any breakfast before coming to the mall. Seemed like they'd be hungry.

"Good question. I'll ask Brising." Freya quickly lifted the coolest of the necklaces she wore—a gorgeous one of hammered gold decorated with small winking jewels. Brising was the name of the shiny walnut-size teardrop-shaped amber jewel dangling from its center. It gave her the power of prophecy.

"Brising, where can we find the best clothes and deals around here?" Freya asked the jewel. Since it always spoke in a low humming sound that only she could understand, Freya listened for a few moments and then repeated aloud what the jewel had said:

> *"Count six doors,*
> *Passing stores.*
> *Find happy rags,*
> *Marked with price tags!"*

"Rags?" echoed Idun. She and Freya looked at each other and burst out laughing.

"Maybe you misunderstood, Brising," Freya told her

jewel. "We're shopping for clothes, not rags." She listened for another few moments, then shrugged. "Brising's gone mum."

"Oh well," said Idun. "Let's go past the next six doors and see what we find."

Appearing amused, Freya lifted an eyebrow. "Looking for more apple-y clothing?"

"Who me?" Idun asked innocently. "Why would you think that?" With a grin, she patted the gold-colored knit hat she wore over her long brown hair. A brown felt "stem" and green felt leaf were stitched to its top, making the entire hat resemble a gold-colored apple.

Freya eyed the hat. "Uh, maybe because you are ever so slightly apple obsessed?"

Idun grinned. "Maybe so. My apples are important." It was true. The apples she tended grew year-round— even in winter snow—in one particular grove in Asgard. Though students often ate them whole, the school's kitchen staff also made them into applesauce and baked goods such as apple turnovers. Or pressed them to make the tasty apple juice served in the school's cafeteria, which was officially called the Valhallateria, or just "the V" for short.

Idun finished her chips and tossed her empty bag into a recycle bin. By now, she and Freya had passed two boot stores, a leather-goods shop, a clock shop, an artisan shop called Wood Goods, and a jewelry store. Suddenly Freya came to a halt. "Cool clothes alert!" she blurted, pointing to a shop across the way. It was called Glad Rags.

"Hey! Brising said '*happy* rags' which is almost the same as 'glad rags.' He must've meant we should try this store," said Idun.

Freya pointed to the motto under the store name on the sign over the door: WE SELL ONE-OF-A-KIND, GENTLY USED CLOTHING. Smaller print below read: NOW ACCEPTING SECOND-HAND CLOTHES FROM GODDESSES, GODS, GIANTS, OR ELVES FOR OUR STOCK.

"Ooh!" Idun said, her face lighting up. "Wouldn't 'one-of-a-kind' describe apple-themed clothes?"

Freya grinned and rolled her eyes merrily. "You, girl, have a one-track mind."

Idun grinned back. Okay, so she definitely *was* a little apple obsessed.

The girls entered the shop. There were numerous racks of clothing inside and just one other customer, who was at the shop's counter. Freya made a beeline for the nearest rack. Expertly she began to flip through its contents. Idun chose the next rack over to search for apple-patterned items.

"Dee-lighted you came shopping here today!" a tiny voice suddenly piped up.

Huh? Idun glanced around. Seeing no one speaking to her, however, she went back to sorting through the clothing on the rack.

"I looove that necklace!" another similar tiny voice said to Freya. More voices chimed in, agreeing.

"Who said that?" Idun and Freya exclaimed at the same time.

"Maybe the clothes?" Idun ventured.

"Got it in one," said a pink sports jersey bearing a giant white number one on its front.

Each time the girls touched additional items of clothing, they were startled to hear more cheerful voices call out to them.

"Hey! Try me on. I guarantee I'll make you look *purr*fect!" said a shirt with a kitten on its front.

"To wear me is to love me," promised a dress with a heart design.

"So happy you are considering me, even if I am a bit flashy!" squealed a top with tiny lights that blinked on and off when touched.

"I guess they really are *glad* rags," Idun quipped.

"Yes, we're cheerful," a fancy ruffled blouse Freya had pulled out agreed. "Because we're all clothes for special occasions. That's what 'glad rags' means!"

Just then the customer at the counter announced, "Ma'am? I want to make a return." Glancing up, Idun watched the customer shove a large bag across the sales counter. After peeking inside the bag, the curly haired shopkeeper on the other side of the counter raised her eyebrows, which were as bushy as the eyebrows of the customer.

"Humans?" Idun mouthed to Freya. Freya nodded, wiggling her own brows to indicate the reason she thought Idun was probably right. This was Midgard, of course, where humans dwelled, and they all had bushy eyebrows.

"Returns are no problem. I'm Ms. Glad, the store owner," replied the woman behind the counter. Her smile was big and cheery. "I'm so *very* pleased you shop here and only sorry that this time your purchase didn't work out for you."

As Idun listened in on the conversation at the counter, she could also hear the jolly pieces of clothing

Freya was rummaging through urging her to try them on and buy them.

"I'll say it didn't work out!" the customer huffed. She pointed to the bag. "There's something downright spooky about that . . . *thing* in there." She lowered her voice so that Idun had to scoot a little closer to hear. "When I put it on last night, it began to tighten around me. And then—and I swear I'm not making this up—it started making these noises. Shrill cries, sort of like seagulls or banshees or something! I took it off at once!"

"A wise move," Ms. Glad said agreeably. She pulled out some coins and handed them over to the woman. "It is never desirable to have one's clothing shriek."

Idun couldn't tell for sure, but it seemed to her that Ms. Glad wasn't at all surprised by what the customer had said. Well, Idun sure was. Clothes that talked cheerfully were one thing. But *shrieking* clothes were quite another. She glanced at the door wondering if she and Freya should skedaddle.

However, Freya seemed not to have overheard the conversation at the counter. "Ymir's eyeballs! Look at this!" she exclaimed just then.

Ymir was a frost giant who'd lived at the beginning of time. Slain by the gods, his various body parts had been used to grow the nine worlds. And for some reason, everyone spoke of those body parts as slang.

Idun turned toward Freya as her friend held up a bulky bright-orange poncho with short rainbow-colored tassels dangling all over it. Both girls burst out laughing at how ugly it was.

"Yeah, I'm glad Ymir's eyeballs can't see that thing. I sort of wish we couldn't either," said Idun, stepping closer to giggle with Freya over the poncho.

"I can definitely believe this orange poncho is 'one of a kind' like the sign says," Freya said to Idun. "Who would want to wear something that made them look like a giant pumpkin?"

"HeLLO! I can hear you! And what's wrong with

pumpkins?" the poncho demanded to know.

Freya sent Idun an *uh-oh, I forgot it could hear us* look. "Do clothes have feelings?" she whispered to Idun.

"Not sure," Idun whispered back. "I would've guessed 'glad' rags could only feel gladness, but that poncho sounds annoyed. Makes sense the owner wouldn't want to call her store 'Annoyed Rags' though."

The girls giggled, but then quickly stopped when they noticed that the poncho seemed to wilt. "Not everyone has the same taste in clothes," Idun reminded it in a kind voice.

Catching on, Freya added, "Right. I'm sure plenty of people are dying for an orange poncho with tassels. If they knew you were in here, they'd be rushing in to buy you."

The poncho turned a happier, brighter shade of orange. "Yes, of course!" it said, all cheery again.

"Do you girls need help finding anything?" Ms. Glad called out after the customer who'd been at the counter hurried out the shop's door empty-handed.

Idun hoped Ms. Glad hadn't overheard her and Freya. What if she thought they were making fun of the clothes in her shop? They weren't! Well, except for the orange poncho, maybe.

"Thanks, but we're okay for now," Freya replied as she started to flip through the clothes on another rack. "Sorry about the small rip in my seam!" an item called out merrily when she touched it. "A giant tried me on and then accidently shape-shifted herself larger. It'd be an easy repair, though!"

Keeping half an eye on Freya, Idun worked her way closer to the counter, her gaze mostly on that customer's returned bag. The comments she'd overheard had left her super curious about its contents. As she edged toward the bag, she did a quick search of two more racks, but found no apple-patterned items.

"Um, actually," Idun said to the owner, when she neared the counter, "Can I see what's in the bag that other customer just returned?"

The owner raised an eyebrow. "If you dare." But then she laughed as if she were only joking.

Or is she? Idun wondered.

Still smiling, Ms. Glad opened the bag and carefully lifted out a cloak. Wow! It was glorious, covered in gleaming horizontally striped brown and white feathers. When she gently shook it out, Idun felt her heart quicken. Though she couldn't have said just why, especially since the cloak was not apple-themed, she immediately wanted it. She reached out to stroke its white-tipped feathers. As soon as she touched them, the cloak spoke up.

"Fly away with me!" it urged her. "We'll be birds of a feather that stick together."

Idun grinned, and that 'wanting' feeling intensified. Who cared if the customer who'd returned it had called it "spooky"? Idun had to have it!

"Fabulous, isn't it?" Ms. Glad said enthusiastically. "Those are falcon feathers, by the way."

"Interesting," said Idun. She reached out, dying to try it on.

Suddenly Freya appeared beside them. "What an unusual cloak," she said, peering down at it.

Unusual as in weird? Idun wondered, suddenly unsure of her own fashion sense.

But then Freya said, "It's quirky, but cool. Look how well made it is. The feathers all line up so that the horizontal bands of color match perfectly." She smiled at Idun. "Definitely one of a kind. And in a good way."

"So you like it?" Idun asked, still a little unsure.

Freya nodded. "Definitely."

"Enough to buy?" Idun pressed. She really wanted the cloak, but she'd like fashion-forward Freya's seal of approval first.

"Maybe," said Freya. She turned toward the shop owner. "How much is it?"

"I can offer it at a very low price," Ms. Glad told her. "Because as wonderful as this cloak is, it's been returned to my shop three times already. I'd really like to see it go to a good home. So if you'll agree to take it on a no-refunds, no-exchanges basis, I'll cut the price in half. You can have it for a hundred kroner."

Freya's pale blue eyes lit up. "Fantastic!" she said excitedly. "That's a bargain. I'll take it!"

Wha–? Idun's face fell. Too late, she realized that she hadn't made it clear that *she* was interested in buying the cloak.

"Hey, thanks for finding it for me," Freya said to Idun as she fished in the pocket of her *hangerock* for coins.

When Idun said nothing, Freya glanced up at her. A look of confusion came into her eyes as she noticed the crestfallen look on Idun's face. "Wait a minute," she said. "Did I make a mistake here? Do you want the cloak?"

Idun hesitated. As much as she did want the falcon feather cloak, she could see that Freya wanted it too. She prided herself on her generosity. It would feel selfish to take the cloak for herself, even if she had seen it first. They hadn't known each other all that long, and she really wanted Freya to like her. It might help seal their new friendship if Idun let her have the cloak.

"Well, I do like it. But you said dibs first. That cloak will look great on you." In the back of her mind she somehow expected Freya to guess how she really felt and say, *No, you should have it.*

Instead, Freya beamed at her. "Really? That's so sweet of you!" She handed over the coins to Ms. Glad.

Upset, but not knowing what to do about it, Idun moved away from the counter as Freya completed her purchase. Turning, she headed for the door, hoping Freya wouldn't guess how unhappy she was. When Idun bumped a sweater with a crystal ball pictured on its front, it happily sing-songed a prediction: "Do a good deed, and you'll get what you need."

"Oh, hush," Idun scolded it. "I did do a good deed and now *Freya* has what I need!"

"Do a good deed, and you'll get what you need," the sweater repeated cheerily. Idun just rolled her eyes. She felt grumpy and somehow cheated out of that cloak, though she knew it wasn't really fair of her to think that.

Moments later, the two girls exited the shop. "I feel bad that you didn't find anything to buy," Freya said, bagged cloak in hand. "We still have time to check out at least one more shop before we meet up with Skade and Sif if you want."

"No, that's okay," Idun replied in as bright a voice as she could manage. She'd lost her chance to own the feather cloak. Nothing else would seem quite as wonderful, even something apple-themed.

That store had been named incorrectly, she decided as they walked away from it. It should've been named Sad Rags or Mad Rags. Because that's how she'd wound up feeling after shopping in there!